Ravenscroft

A Play

by Don Nigro

A SAMUEL FRENCH ACTING EDITION

SAMUEL FRENCH

FOUNDED 1830

SAMUELFRENCH.COM

IMPORTANT BILLING AND CREDIT REQUIREMENTS

All producers of RAVENSCROFT *must* give credit to the Author of the Play in all programs distributed in connection with performances of the Play and in all instances in which the title of the Play appears for purposes of advertising, publicizing or otherwise exploiting the Play and/or a production. The name of the Author *must* also appear on a separate line, on which no other name appears, immediately following the title, and *must* appear in size of type not less than fifty percent the size of the title type.

CHARACTERS

Ruffing, an Inspector (40)

Marcy, a governess (25)

Mrs. Ravenscroft (35)

Gillian, her daughter (17)

Dolly, the maid (20)

Mrs. French, the housekeeper (38)

PLACE

A remote manor house in a rural English county in December of the year 1905.

ACT I

SETTING: The unit set is quite simple—a desk, a couch, a leather chair, some wooden chairs, some books and a place for liquor. The furniture is real, but the library in which Inspector Ruffing will spend the entire play is not defined by walls but by light, and the five women, who will also be onstage and visible for the entire play, will seat themselves in the shadows at various locations upstage and elsewhere as the Inspector questions someone else. The effect is that the women move into the light when they are actually in the room with him, and move out of the light but not out of our sight when they have left the library. Thus they are always, quite literally, at the edge of his—and our—consciousness during the play, and may move back into focus instantly simply by moving into the light. No one is ever frozen in place, nor is any player ever out of character. The transitions are thus extremely fluid, the scenes move easily from one to the other and characters may linger in the light for a moment after the next scene has begun. Thus there is no space between scenes and there are no blackouts. Under no circumstances should this play ever be done with walls, doors, and a conventional box set. To move into the light is to move to the forefront of Ruffing's consciousness. To move out of it is to move out of focus, but never to leave it altogether. The way the play moves is always a part of the play.

"Thinke but how deare you bought
       This same which you have caught,
Such thoughts will make you more in love
       with truth."
                              —Ben Jonson

AT RISE: Ticking CLOCK. LIGHTS slowly up on the library and surrounding shadows. MARCY is down right, looking downstage through an invisible window. RUFFING is behind her, also standing. The other four WOMEN are seated on various pieces of furniture upstage and elsewhere, in the shadows, clearly visible but out of the light.

RUFFING. I'm afraid I'm going to have to ask a few questions.

MARCY. It's begun to snow.

RUFFING. Miss Kleiner? Are you listening?

MARCY. Yes. But not to you. Why are you afraid?

RUFFING. I beg your pardon?

MARCY. You said you were afraid to ask questions.

RUFFING. No, I said I was afraid I'm going to have to ask you—

MARCY. There, you said it again.

RUFFING. That's a polite apology for the inconvenience, not an admission of terror.

MARCY. So you're not afraid to ask questions? You like asking questions?

RUFFING. It's my job to ask questions. That's what police inspectors do.

MARCY. And why is that?

RUFFING. Because we need to find the truth, of course.

MARCY. Why do we need to find the truth?

RUFFING. So that people who commit crimes will be apprehended and punished.

MARCY. And why must they be apprehended and punished?

RUFFING. Miss Kleiner, we're wasting time.

MARCY. So when I ask questions, it's a waste of time, but when you ask questions, it's not?

RUFFING. Your job is not to ask questions, your job is to answer the questions, all right?

MARCY. Is it? Is it all right?

RUFFING. You work as governess here?

MARCY. If you're concerned about wasting time, why do you ask a question to which you already know the answer?

RUFFING. I would take this matter a little more seriously if I were you, Miss Kleiner.

MARCY. Why would you do that?

RUFFING. Because a man is dead.

MARCY. Yes, well, that's fairly serious, that's a rather serious thing, I'll grant you. Yes, Inspector, I work as a governess and companion to Gillian, Miss Ravenscroft.

RUFFING. Can you tell me what happened here?

MARCY. Patrick Roarke attacked me, and I pushed him away. He fell down the staircase and was killed.

RUFFING. He attacked you at the top of the staircase?

MARCY. He tried to force his way into my room. I ran from him. He caught me at the top of the staircase and I pushed him away. He lost his balance and fell.

RUFFING. Why did you open your door to him in the first place?

MARCY. I didn't open my door to him. I'd just paid a visit to Gillian's room. She hadn't been feeling well, and I looked in to see that she was all right. She was sleeping. I sat with her for a moment—not long, it was cold, and I was just in my nightgown.

RUFFING. Is it your usual habit to move about the house in your nightgown?

MARCY. My room is just across the hall from Gillian's. It was late. Patrick was not permitted upstairs. The rest of us in the house are women. It was not uncommon for me to check on Gillian in the night. She has bad dreams, now and then. It was just for a few moments.

RUFFING. But on that particular night, Patrick WAS upstairs.

MARCY. Yes.

RUFFING. Do you know why?

MARCY. No.

RUFFING. You don't think he came upstairs with the specific intention of assaulting you?

MARCY. I don't know.

RUFFING. Where was he when you came out of Gillian's room?

MARCY. It was dark in the hall. He must have been waiting in the shadows. I was just about to open the door of my room when I felt him grab hold of me.

RUFFING. Did you cry out?

MARCY. He put his hand over my mouth and told me not to. He was a very strong man. I struggled to get away, and somehow I managed to elude him for a moment. I ran for the stairs.

RUFFING. Did you call for help then?

MARCY. It happened very quickly. I was frightened. I just wanted to get away.

RUFFING. Had Patrick made advances towards you before this?

MARCY. No. Well, yes, a few times.

RUFFING. And what happened on those occasions?

MARCY. On those occasions I got away from him.

RUFFING. Did you report these incidents to Mrs. Ravenscroft?

MARCY. No.

RUFFING. Why not?

MARCY. I didn't want to bother her with such things. I didn't think at the time that it was a very serious problem. He was not violent. I thought I could deal with it myself.

RUFFING. And you told no one?

MARCY. No.

RUFFING. I find that rather hard to believe.

MARCY. Do you? Why is that?

RUFFING. It might be construed, if this incident should result in some formal charge leading to a trial, it might be construed from the fact that you did not report this man's previous advances towards you, that these advances were not entirely unwelcome.

MARCY. It is not my business to regulate the unwarranted presumptions of foul-minded cretins.

RUFFING. Then please tell me why you did not report these incidents to Mrs. Ravenscroft.

MARCY. I was afraid of losing my position.

RUFFING. How could you lose your position by merely reporting the unacceptable behavior of another employee?

MARCY. Because Patrick would very likely have told Mrs. Ravenscroft that— This whole conversation is extremely distasteful to me.

RUFFING. Told her what?

MARCY. That I'd encouraged his advances, perhaps even that I'd attempted to seduce him, that I was in fact the strumpet your hypothetical idiotic juryman might presume I was.

RUFFING. And how much of that was true?

MARCY. None of it was true.

RUFFING. Then why were you so afraid to speak?

MARCY. I didn't know which of us she'd believe. Patrick had been here much longer than I, and he was a very accomplished—talker. And a very charming man. He was the sort of man who could convince just about anyone of just about anything, if he put his mind to it.

RUFFING. But he couldn't convince you to become his mistress?

MARCY. No.

RUFFING. You seem to have very little respect for Mrs. Ravenscroft's intelligence.

MARCY. Have you ever worked in domestic employment, Inspector?

RUFFING. Of course not.

MARCY. Then you don't understand anything about it, do you?

RUFFING. Don't take that tone with me.

MARCY. You've taken a very superior tone with me.

RUFFING. You are a suspect in a murder investigation.

MARCY. It was not a murder, it was an accident. I'm alone in a strange country. I have no money and no place to go. I'm completely at the mercy of my employers, and apparently also of officious bullies like yourself.

RUFFING. A strange country?

MARCY. I was born in Vienna.

RUFFING. You speak very good English.

MARCY. My mother was American. I speak English, German, French and Italian.

RUFFING. That's very impressive. How did an accomplished young woman like you come to be working here?

MARCY. Mrs. Ravenscroft's late husband was friendly with the local priest here, who was a friend of the Mother Superior of the convent in Austria where I lived before I came here. They wanted a young person who could teach their daughter languages and be a companion for her.

RUFFING. You were a nun?

MARCY. No. I stayed at the convent between employments elsewhere. The sisters were very kind to me.

RUFFING. And before that?

MARCY. Before that I was a governess in Vienna.

RUFFING. Why did you leave your previous employment?

MARCY. I was no longer required. May I go now? I'm very tired.

RUFFING. I'll want to speak with you again, after I've seen the others.

MARCY. I'm sure you will. Excuse me.

RUFFING. Miss Kleiner?

MARCY. Yes?

RUFFING. It was not my intention to insult you, or to upset you in any way. I know this is difficult, but I have my job to do. I hope you understand that.

MARCY. Am I excused?
RUFFING. Yes.
MARCY. How nice.

(SHE moves out of the light and sits in the shadows. RUFFING stands there, thinking, as MRS. RAVENSCROFT moves into the light.)

MRS. RAVENSCROFT. I do hope you haven't upset poor Marcy. She's a frail little thing, and she's had such a terrible experience. Good Lord, look at the snow come down. You're going to have a time of it getting home tonight, Inspector.
RUFFING. Mrs. Ravenscroft, how long has Miss Kleiner been employed by you?
MRS. RAVENSCROFT. Marcy's been here six months.

(DOLLY moves into the light and looks at them nervously.)

MRS. RAVENSCROFT. I think it's six months. Is it six months, Dolly?
DOLLY. Yes, mum. I don't know, mum. I think so.
RUFFING. Has her work been satisfactory?
MRS. RAVENSCROFT. I suppose so. What is it, Dolly?
DOLLY. Would you like tea, mum?
MRS. RAVENSCROFT. Tea, Inspector?
RUFFING. No, thank you. Nothing for me.
MRS. RAVENSCROFT. Nothing for us, thank you, Dolly, unless the Inspector would like a little crumpet.

RUFFING. Just satisfactory?

MRS. RAVENSCROFT. No, they're excellent crumpets. Mrs. French makes them.

RUFFING. I was speaking of Miss Kleiner.

MRS. RAVENSCROFT. No, I don't think Marcy makes crumpets. She did make a wonderful hot strudel once. She's Viennese, you know. Dolly, do you recall Marcy's strudel?

DOLLY. Yes, mum. I do. Very sticky.

MRS. RAVENSCROFT. Would you like some strudel, Inspector?

DOLLY. We don't have any strudel, mum.

MRS. RAVENSCROFT. But I'm certain Marcy could whip up her strudel, if the Inspector wants it that badly.

RUFFING. I don't want any strudel, thank you.

MRS. RAVENSCROFT. I appreciate that, Inspector, because, to tell you the truth, in her present state, I couldn't promise you her strudel would come out quite as nicely as it might otherwise. Is there something else you wanted, Dolly?

DOLLY. No, mum.

MRS. RAVENSCROFT. Well, then, don't stand there like a wooden Indian, go and get the crumpets. No, never mind, just ask Marcy if she and Gillian want something.

DOLLY. Yes, mum. Thank you, mum. (*SHE moves out of the light.*)

MRS. RAVENSCROFT. She's really a very stupid girl.

RUFFING. I thought she spoke four languages.

MRS. RAVENSCROFT. Dolly? Why, she can barely speak English.

RUFFING. I mean Miss Kleiner.

MRS. RAVENSCROFT. Then say what you mean, Inspector, don't fiddle about the bush. Her father was kicked in the head by a horse.

RUFFING. In Vienna?

MRS. RAVENSCROFT. In the barn. Oh, you mean Marcy. No, I don't think her people had horses. Her father was some sort of artist or something. She's a sweet creature, but I suspect now and then that she's feeble-minded. I mean Dolly. Marcy's not feeble-minded, she speaks four languages. Of course, my husband was a linguist at Oxford, and he wasn't very bright at all. But Marcy really is bright, I like a bright woman, within limits at least, don't you?

RUFFING. Have you ever had cause to complain of Miss Kleiner's conduct here?

MRS. RAVENSCROFT. My daughter has become very attached to her. She seems to be a good teacher and a pleasant companion. I suppose I can't say that I've had any real reason to complain.

RUFFING. I detect that you have some reservations.

MRS. RAVENSCROFT. Yes, I was going to London for the weekend, but I cancelled when all this happened.

RUFFING. I mean reservations about Miss Kleiner.

MRS. RAVENSCROFT. No, I have no reservations about Marcy.

RUFFING. How long had Patrick worked for you?

MRS. RAVENSCROFT. Since old Bemis was kicked in the head by the gelding. Dolly's father. After that, he took it into his head that he was Jack the Ripper's son by Queen Victoria. We had to have him shot. The gelding. Put him out of his misery. That's no life for a horse.

Bemis we put in the attic, and got Patrick. That would be, oh, ten or eleven years ago. I remember it was snowing.

RUFFING. What were Patrick's duties here?

MRS. RAVENSCROFT. Coachman, groom, footman, repairman, gardener. He did all the heavy work. He did a wonderful job with my aspidistra. Would you like to see it?

RUFFING. Sounds like a handy fellow to have around.

MRS. RAVENSCROFT. Yes, he was good at everything he put his hand to.

RUFFING. Did you have any indication he was behaving in an indecent way with the help?

MRS. FRENCH. (*Moving into the light.*) Excuse me, mum, would you like me to put on the roast?

MRS. RAVENSCROFT. Will you be staying for supper, Inspector?

RUFFING. No, thank you.

MRS. RAVENSCROFT. Yes, do start it, Mrs. French, I have a feeling we'll all be needing meat soon.

MRS. FRENCH. Yes, mum. (*SHE looks at Ruffing and moves out of the light.*)

RUFFING. Well, did you?

MRS. RAVENSCROFT. Did I what?

RUFFING. Did you suspect that Patrick might be misbehaving with the help?

MRS. RAVENSCROFT. He was a charming young man. I expect Dolly had some sort of an infatuation with him, she's an awfully silly girl. But it was nothing serious, I'm certain.

RUFFING. But this was by all accounts a handsome, well-put-together young man in his twenty-ninth year. He must have had some sort of female companionship.

MRS. RAVENSCROFT. Oh, he was quite popular with many of the village girls, I think, but I had no sign from his behavior here that he would ever assault any woman, certainly not in the house. He was too good looking to have to force his attentions. If he had, I'd have hauled him on the carpet.

RUFFING. What happened the night he died?

MRS. RAVENSCROFT. I retired about ten. I read in bed for twenty minutes or so, Byron, I think, or Rossetti, something wicked. Gives me pleasant dreams. Then I put out the light and went to sleep. I drop off right away, it's a gift I've always had, used to infuriate my husband. I was awakened some time later by a commotion in the hall. I put on my dressing gown, went out into the corridor and found Marcy at the top of the stairs, and poor Patrick lying at the bottom like a rag doll. I called for Mrs. French, and went down the steps, but poor Patrick appeared to be quite dead. His neck seemed to be broken. I sent Dolly for the doctor, I'm sure he could verify—

RUFFING. Yes, I've spoken to the doctor. What did Miss Kleiner say to you about what had happened?

MRS. RAVENSCROFT. At first she didn't say anything. She stood there at the top of the steps for the longest time. Then my daughter came out of her room. Marcy tried to keep her from seeing Patrick, but Gillian must have seen him, for she began to be quite upset. She's only seventeen, and it was a very shocking thing to look at—he was twisted grotesquely and staring up—it was horrible. Then Marcy took Gillian back into her room. I left Mrs. French with the body and went back up the steps to see my daughter.

RUFFING. Did you ask Marcy what happened?

MRS. RAVENSCROFT. She said it was an accident.

RUFFING. She mentioned nothing about Patrick assaulting her?

MRS. RAVENSCROFT. Not in front of Gillian. She did later, when she and I were alone.

RUFFING. And what exactly did she say to you?

MRS. RAVENSCROFT. She said Patrick tried to push her into her bedroom, that she'd struggled and run away from him, that he'd caught her at the top of the staircase and in the struggle he lost his balance and fell. I'm afraid that's all I know about it.

RUFFING. Did you believe what she told you?

MRS. RAVENSCROFT. I saw no reason not to. Don't you?

RUFFING. But you just said you don't believe Patrick would assault a woman.

MRS. RAVENSCROFT. The fact is, Patrick smelled of liquor when I found him. He'd been known to take a drink now and then, and I'd warned him that if he drank on duty, I'd let him go. I never saw him drinking again. Perhaps he drank after we all went to bed. It seems possible to me that, under the influence of alcohol, he might behave in a manner more bold than he would dare to when sober. And Marcy is a very beautiful young woman. Certainly you've noticed.

RUFFING. (*Thinking about it for a moment.*) Do you think I might have a word with your daughter?

MRS. RAVENSCROFT. I'd prefer you didn't. She's still very upset.

RUFFING. I must interview everyone in the house, and the sooner the better.

MRS. RAVENSCROFT. Well. If you must, you must. But do be careful with her. She's a rather—delicate girl. You will be gentle with her, won't you? You seem like a gentle man.

(GILLIAN moves into the light. MRS. RAVENSCROFT moves past her, exchanging a look, and then into the shadows.)

RUFFING. Miss Ravenscroft, can you tell me what happened here last night?

GILLIAN. Patrick died.

RUFFING. Yes, but what did you hear, and what did you see?

GILLIAN. Haven't they told you?

RUFFING. I've spoken to your mother and to Miss Kleiner, but I need to hear separately from each of you.

GILLIAN. Why? Do you think they're lying?

RUFFING. It's a procedure I have to follow.

GILLIAN. But why?

RUFFING. That's just how we do it.

GILLIAN It happened the way they say it did.

RUFFING. You were in your room?

GILLIAN. Whatever they say.

RUFFING. Miss Ravenscroft—

GILLIAN. My name is Gillian. What's your name?

RUFFING. Inspector Ruffing.

GILLIAN. No, that's what we're supposed to call you, but what's your name, really?

RUFFING. My name is John.

GILLIAN. Then when they're not around telling us what to do and what to say and what to call each other, I'll call you John, and you call me Gillian, and we'll be more like real people to one another, all right? I much prefer it that way.

RUFFING. All right.

GILLIAN. Are you married, John?

RUFFING. My wife is dead.

GILLIAN. I know what that's like. My father is dead.

RUFFING. When did your father die?

GILLIAN. September.

RUFFING. September of this year?

GILLIAN. Yes.

RUFFING. I'm sorry, I didn't realize it was so recently.

GILLIAN. When did your wife die?

RUFFING. Four years ago.

GILLIAN. Do you have children?

RUFFING. I have a daughter, just your age.

GILLIAN. What's her name?

RUFFING. Mary.

GILLIAN. Does she look like you?

RUFFING. She looks like her mother.

GILLIAN. Do you have her picture?

RUFFING. Yes, I do. Here. (*HE takes out his pocket watch and opens it.*) This is my wife, and my daughter when she was thirteen. It was taken just before my wife's death.

GILLIAN. How beautiful they are. What did she die of?

RUFFING. Complications after childbirth. A few weeks after.

GILLIAN. Oh. And the child, too, I suppose. I mean, she doesn't look at all pregnant here, and the baby isn't in the picture.

RUFFING. Yes. That's right. You're a very observant girl.

GILLIAN. Did she know she was going to die?

RUFFING. I believe she did, yes. She wanted to have the picture taken with our daughter, so I would have it.

GILLIAN. She loved you.

RUFFING. So you see, I do understand something about how you feel.

GILLIAN. Maybe.

RUFFING. Were you fond of Patrick?

GILLIAN. Patrick was very funny. He had a knack for making women happy. He also had a knack for making them unhappy. I suppose the two go together. I mean, the one tends to lead more or less inevitably to the other.

RUFFING. Did he ever make you unhappy?

GILLIAN. Everybody makes you unhappy sometime or other. We were good friends.

RUFFING. Did Patrick also have other good friends in the house? Was he friends with Miss Kleiner?

GILLIAN. He liked her a lot. We all do. We all love Marcy. Except perhaps for Mrs. French and Mother, but it's hard to tell sometimes what Mother loves. She's tricky that way. I think Marcy is the most beautiful woman I've ever seen. Don't you?

RUFFING. Did you hear anything last night, before you came out of your room?

GILLIAN. You don't really want to be my friend, you just want to find things out. I don't think that's very nice. I especially don't think it's nice to use your daughter and your poor dead wife and child to get on my good side.

RUFFING. Now look here, Gillian. You asked me about them and I told you. And I'd be very happy to be your friend, but a person has died here, and I've got to be certain just what happened.

GILLIAN. Why?

RUFFING. Because that's the law.

GILLIAN. And the law, of course, is a lot more important than a real, living person like me.

RUFFING. Patrick was a living person, too, and now he's dead. The law is there to protect everybody. We need to make sure how it happened so people can't just go around pushing people down stairs when they feel like it. So did you hear anything or didn't you?

GILLIAN. No.

RUFFING. But you must have heard something. Otherwise, why would you come out of your room?

GILLIAN. Well, that makes sense. I suppose I must have heard something, perhaps the sound of Patrick clattering down the steps. It must have made a frightful racket, with his boots and all. He was always polishing his boots, he was quite vain about them. I expect they'll bury him in them. Seems like a waste of good shoe leather to me. I mean, a perfectly good cow died for those boots.

RUFFING. Miss Kleiner had just left your room?

GILLIAN. When?

RUFFING. When you heard the noise.

GILLIAN. Is that what she told you?

RUFFING. Was she in your room or wasn't she?

GILLIAN. If she says she was, then she must have been.

RUFFING. But you didn't see her?

GILLIAN. Maybe I was asleep. What are they going to do to her? They wouldn't hang her, would they? It seems like a crime to kill someone so beautiful.

RUFFING. Why would they hang her?

GILLIAN. For murdering Patrick, of course.

RUFFING. Is that what happened?

GILLIAN. Isn't that what you think?

RUFFING. What do you think?

GILLIAN. I'm a young lady, I'm not supposed to think, that's frowned upon in my circle.

RUFFING. Oh, come on, you're a smart girl, you have your own thoughts, what are they?

GILLIAN. I think the ghost killed him.

RUFFING. The ghost?

GILLIAN. Didn't they tell you? No, of course they didn't. Our house is haunted. It's true, we live in a very haunted house. The ghost killed my father, too. Then she killed Patrick.

RUFFING. This ghost is a woman, is it?

GILLIAN. Oh, yes. I've seen her. You'd best be careful, Inspector. She seems to fancy good looking men.

RUFFING. Gillian, this is not a game, this is an adult matter, and a very serious one, and you must speak to me like one adult to another. You musn't waste my time with childish stories about ghosts, so stop this nonsense and tell me the truth.

GILLIAN. Of course. I'm just teasing you. It happened exactly the way they told you. Whatever they said. You ARE staying for supper, aren't you? Mrs. French is a wonderful cook, she hardly ever poisons anybody she likes. And you're such a nice man, I like you, and I think you're not nearly as stuffy as you think you ought to be. I wouldn't want anything bad to happen to you. What would your poor lovely daughter Mary do then, without her handsome daddy? She'd be an orphan. I wish I was. Look at the snow. I love the snow, don't you? This is my very favorite time of year. (*SHE looks out the window.*)

(*RUFFING looks at her, very troubled. MRS. RAVENSCROFT moves into the light, and GILLIAN moves into the shadows.*)

RUFFING. Mrs. Ravenscroft, is your daughter—I don't know exactly how to phrase this question. You said she was—delicate, I believe, was the word you used. Did you mean physically, or in other respects as well?

MRS. RAVENSCROFT. Other respects?

RUFFING. She's been speaking to me about ghosts.

MRS. RAVENSCROFT. What about them?

RUFFING. She says a ghost killed Patrick Roarke.

MRS. RAVENSCROFT. And you believe that?

RUFFING. Of course I don't believe it, but I do find it extremely odd that a girl of seventeen should be telling such a thing to a police inspector. She's not really a child any more, and—

MRS. RAVENSCROFT. Ah, but you see, she is. And she isn't. Inspector, my daughter has had more than one emotional upset in her life. Nothing too terrible, she just—she demonstrates on occasion an inability to distinguish between fantasy and reality. She's been much better since Marcy came to live with us. Whatever else you may say about her, Marcy is a person with a very clear sense of reality, and I noticed right away that it seemed to be rubbing off on Gillian. They've been very close. It was partly, I think, her father's death that upset her so much.

RUFFING. But Marcy arrived six months ago.

MRS. RAVENSCROFT. Yes, it was June, the honeysuckle was in bloom. She looked so beautiful out there on the lawn, with the honeysuckle behind her. I think that's why my husband hired her, she looked decidedly Pre-Raphaelite, his favorite period. Of course, he was always taking in strays of one sort or another.

RUFFING. But your husband died in September.

MRS. RAVENSCROFT. Yes.

RUFFING. So it couldn't have been your husband's death that caused your daughter's emotional problems.

MRS. RAVENSCROFT. No, it just made them worse. That's why we hired Marcy.

RUFFING. But you hired Marcy three months before your husband died.

MRS. RAVENSCROFT. So?

RUFFING. So when did these emotional problems first appear?

MRS. RAVENSCROFT. I think you're making entirely too much of this, Inspector. She's not a bad girl, she just plays with people now and then, it's a kind of game, really.

RUFFING. She plays with people?

MRS. RAVENSCROFT. Yes. She's playful. It's quite harmless.

RUFFING. Is she often playful with the truth?

MRS. RAVENSCROFT. She can be.

RUFFING. In other words, she's a liar.

MRS. RAVENSCROFT. Oh, no, she wouldn't lie, she never lies, exactly, she just—interprets reality somewhat more creatively than most people, in her own way, for her own amusement.

RUFFING. Have you sought professional help for your daughter?

MRS. RAVENSCROFT. She doesn't need professional help. You're seeing her at a very extraordinary time. First her father, then Patrick. She was so fond of Patrick. He was like her big brother. I hope there will be no need to upset her further about this. You really must stay for supper, Inspector. We have so much food in the house, and now Patrick's not here to eat most of it. He had such a tremendous appetite, it's amazing how he kept in such good shape. There wasn't an ounce of fat on his body, not one ounce, anywhere. I suppose it was all the exercise he got. Barbells. He lifted them.

RUFFING. How did your husband die?

MRS. RAVENSCROFT. My husband?

RUFFING. Yes. How did he die?

MRS. RAVENSCROFT. He fell down the steps.

RUFFING. He fell down the steps?

MRS. RAVENSCROFT. I'm afraid so.

RUFFING. The same steps?

MRS. RAVENSCROFT. Yes.

RUFFING. Just like Patrick?

MRS. RAVENSCROFT. Yes. Well, no, not JUST like him. My husband did not lift barbells. And Patrick was pushed, whereas my husband simply fell.

RUFFING. Let me get this straight. Within three months, two men in a household are found dead at the bottom of the same staircase and no one has bothered to inform me of this?

MRS. RAVENSCROFT. I believe I just did. I think it was me. It must have been me. I recognized my voice.

You've really got to start paying more attention, Inspector. If you don't, who will?

RUFFING. Are you trying to hide something from me?

MRS. RAVENSCROFT. Not that I know of. You'll have to forgive me if my husband's recent headlong plunge down the main staircase is not one of my favorite topics of conversation.

RUFFING. I can understand that, but still I think it extremely odd that nobody took the trouble to tell me about it. Even the doctor said nothing about it.

MRS. RAVENSCROFT. Probably he didn't know. He's new here. It was another doctor, dear old Docky Witherspoon, who attended my husband.

RUFFING. Why did you change doctors?

MRS. RAVENSCROFT. We had very little choice. Doctor Witherspoon died.

RUFFING. I hope he didn't fall down your staircase.

MRS. RAVENSCROFT. No, I believe he choked on something. The man was ninety-one years old, Inspector. Good Lord, you don't think we're going about throwing all the men in the immediate vicinity head first down our staircase, do you?

RUFFING. This is getting rather more complex than I had at first anticipated.

MRS. RAVENSCROFT. Yes, well, life has a tendency to do that, doesn't it? Surely you've found that, in your line of work. Excuse me, I've got to go make sure Mrs. French hasn't fallen asleep over the pot roast.

RUFFING. Mrs. Ravenscroft, I checked the files of my predecessor, Inspector McCullough, before I came out here, and there is no mention whatsoever of your husband's death.

MRS. RAVENSCROFT. Well, old Bertie McCullough was a sweet man, but he was rather inefficient. Getting on in years, a shade absentminded, and in any case I don't know what there was to put in a file, it was so clearly an accident. If you have any questions about it, why don't you just ring up old Bertie and ask him? Of course, you might have some trouble getting a hold of him. He retired to Scotland, one of those remote islands. Lord knows why he'd want to do that, but then, Lord knows why a Scotsman wants to wear those little skirts, either. I don't know why we pursue loneliness like we do. There's quite enough of it going around as is, without us having to seek it out and hoard it up like pieces of eight. What's that smell? Do you smell that? Dolly? DOLLY. Where is that girl? She's got a head like an eggplant. DOLLY.

DOLLY. (*Moving into the light, somewhat distraught.*) Yes, mum?

MRS. RAVENSCROFT. What are you doing in there? Burning the meat?

DOLLY. Oh, no, mum. We're burning the gravy.

MRS. RAVENSCROFT. Ah, well, that's all right, then, I suppose. If you'll excuse me, Inspector, I must go and supervise the ritual burning of the gravy. I hope you can amuse yourself in some way while I'm gone. Come along, Dolly. (*SHE moves upstage and into the shadows.*)

(*DOLLY remains in the light a moment, looking at the Inspector.*)

DOLLY. Inspector—
RUFFING. Yes? What is it, Dolly?
DOLLY. I, uh, I—

MRS. RAVENSCROFT. (*Shouting, from the shadows.*) Dolly, why is the pudding on the floor?

DOLLY. I put it there to cool, mum. There's a nice draft down there.

MRS. RAVENSCROFT. Well, it must be cool enough, because the cat's eating it.

DOLLY. Oh, dear. Excuse me, sir.

RUFFING. Was there something you wanted to say to me?

DOLLY. I, uh, only wished to enquire, sir, if you liked your, um, pudding on your, you know, plate, sir, or if you liked it, you know, um, in a—glass.

RUFFING. In a glass?

MRS. RAVENSCROFT. Dolly, get your wretched wiggly little bum down here.

DOLLY. Excuse me, sir, if I don't go, she'll kill me. Well, I don't mean actually kill me. I was speaking, you know, metaphysically.

RUFFING. You mean metaphorically?

DOLLY. Whatever you say.

(*SHE rushes into the shadows. MARCY moves into the light.*)

RUFFING. Miss Kleiner, how would you describe the mental state of Miss Ravenscroft?

MARCY. Miss or Mrs.?

RUFFING. Miss.

MARCY. Gillian's led a much too sheltered life here. Her father spoiled her a bit, and I suppose her mother did too, in a way. She's a very creative person—she writes, paints, draws, plays the piano beautifully, she does everything well and rather effortlessly—

RUFFING. Does she lie?

MARCY. Not exactly.

RUFFING. What does that mean?

MARCY. She's not a willful liar, but she has a vivid imagination. That's the best I can do. You can't hope to understand someone as complicated as Gillian, or anybody, for that matter, on the basis of a few conversations. Life is more complex than that. Do you think she's lied to you?

RUFFING. I found her answers to be at best unsatisfactory and in some ways bizarre.

MARCY. What did she tell you?

RUFFING. She seemed willing to confirm whatever you and Mrs. Ravenscroft said, without hearing what it was, as though—

MARCY. As though she'd been told to keep her mouth shut? That's an interesting theory, Inspector, but if you knew her better, you'd realize that Gillian always says exactly what she feels like, no matter what anyone tells her.

RUFFING. Has she ever spoken to you about ghosts?

MARCY. Ghosts? Oh, Inspector, I'm afraid she's been teasing you.

RUFFING. Teasing me? I'm conducting a murder investigation and she's teasing me?

MARCY. Are you accusing me of murder?

RUFFING. I'm attempting to ascertain the truth, and I got the distinct impression that she was trying to conceal something from me.

MARCY. She gives everyone that impression. It's just the way she deals with the world. She loves to appear to know something you don't. She's playing.

RUFFING. Well, I'm not.

MARCY. Neither am I.

RUFFING. You don't think she's actually so out of touch with reality that she seriously believes a ghost killed Patrick?

MARCY. If a spirit killed Patrick, it's the kind you drink from a bottle.

RUFFING. Do you know why Patrick would be drinking that much after he'd been warned it could cost him his job?

MARCY. I don't know. He told me not long before that he'd given up drinking for good, because he couldn't handle it, which seemed to me quite a remarkable admission for an Irishman.

RUFFING. So you did have personal conversations with him?

MARCY. Sometimes, yes.

RUFFING. You mean when he wasn't attempting to assault you?

MARCY. Before he began bothering me that way, we were friendly enough.

RUFFING. Just how friendly were you?

MARCY. I was aware that he liked me long before I suspected he'd actually try to do anything against my will. He called me the Viennese Princess. He was always asking me questions about my past, he was a very curious man, rather like you in that respect. He said that he and I had a lot in common—we were both enslaved by the upper classes, both exiles in a strange country, both very fond of

Gillian. He could really be very nice, when he wanted to be. He was certainly not a monster of any sort.

RUFFING. So at one time you did encourage his advances?

MARCY. No, at one time I enjoyed his conversation. When he began to make advances, I pulled back.

RUFFING. So you were playing with him.

MARCY. Why do you insist on making everything sound dirty?

RUFFING. When you began pulling back, is that when he started drinking heavily?

MARCY. No, that wasn't the reason. Perhaps it was that he'd begun seeing things moving about the house at night.

RUFFING. You mean Gillian's ghosts?

MARCY. He was very superstitious, for all his apparent cheek, and he seemed to be under the odd delusion—you'll think this ridiculous—he thought there was some sort of phantom lady who would appear at the top of the staircase from time to time.

RUFFING. That IS ridiculous.

MARCY. I know it's ridiculous, I'm just telling you what he believed, or seemed to believe. Sometimes Patrick could deceive you about his feelings. He was a born storyteller, a kind of actor, really. He should have gone into that, he'd have been very good. I think that's partly why he got on so famously with Gillian—they were alike in that way.

RUFFING. Was it Patrick who put the idea of ghosts into Gillian's head?

MARCY. I don't know. Maybe she put it into his. He'd been here since she was six years old. They were quite easy with one another.

RUFFING. How well did you know the late Mr. Ravenscroft?

MARCY. Not very well.

RUFFING. Why didn't you tell me he'd fallen down the staircase?

MARCY. I presumed you knew.

RUFFING. Was Mr. Ravenscroft kind to you?

MARCY. Yes. Most of the time.

RUFFING. Not all of the time?

MARCY. No one is kind all of the time.

RUFFING. On what occasions was he not kind to you?

MARCY. When he was drinking.

RUFFING. Mr. Ravenscroft had a drinking problem, too?

MARCY. I didn't say he had a problem, I said he drank. Don't you drink?

RUFFING. But you said he was unkind when he drank. Isn't that a problem? Was Mr. Ravenscroft drinking when he fell down the stairs?

MARCY. That's quite possible.

RUFFING. Did HE ever make any advances towards you?

MARCY. No.

RUFFING. But he was not always kind to you.

MARCY. Sometimes when he was drinking he was verbally abusive to everyone, me included. He would now and then get angry and lash out at people.

RUFFING. You didn't like Mr. Ravenscroft?

MARCY. Yes, I liked him.

RUFFING. Even though he was verbally abusive to you?

MARCY. I understood his unhappiness.

RUFFING. What was he unhappy about?

MARCY. I don't know.

RUFFING. But you said you understood it.

MARCY. I understood that he was unhappy. I can recognize profound unhappiness when I see it. I didn't mean I understood exactly why he was unhappy.

RUFFING. Was there trouble in his marriage?

MARCY. I don't think gossiping about my employers is an activity I should be engaging in.

RUFFING. Neither is murder.

MARCY. I haven't murdered anybody. I just pushed him away. I didn't even push him hard. Am I not allowed to defend myself? Just because I'm not one of these damned rich people am I to be treated as if I had no rights at all?

RUFFING. You have a temper, Miss Kleiner.

MARCY. Is it a crime in this country for the hired help to have emotions?

RUFFING. You don't like rich people?

MARCY. I don't like being poor. Can they execute me for that?

RUFFING. They can execute you for murder.

MARCY. I am NOT a murderer.

RUFFING. Then you have no reason to be upset.

MARCY. I have every reason to be upset. You're upsetting me on purpose, in fact, to see what I'll say. Well, if you think you can bully me into some sort of hysterical confession that will make everybody feel better, you're very much mistaken.

(SHE goes upstage and out of the light, with her back to him, as GILLIAN moves into the light.)

RUFFING. Was it Patrick who put the idea of ghosts in your head?

GILLIAN. No. Well, he did tell me stories, when I was a little girl, when he first came to work here. He'd take me on pony rides and let me keep him company while he worked.

RUFFING. Did he tell you stories about ghosts at the top of the staircase?

GILLIAN. These ghosts are real. I saw them.

RUFFING. When did you see them?

GILLIAN. The first time was several years ago. It was a woman, a very dim figure, moving about in the hallway, and then coming to the landing to look down. Then later, I saw another figure with her, and something happened, at the top of the stairs, I don't know what, exactly.

RUFFING. Did you tell Patrick about this?

GILLIAN. Yes.

RUFFING. Did he believe you?

GILLIAN. He told me to leave them alone, and they'd leave me alone. He said the English had never properly learned to mind their own business. But later on I noticed that his attitude towards them seemed to change.

RUFFING. How do you mean?

GILLIAN. He'd started seeing them himself. He had a theory about them, too. He said a ghost is an emotion felt by somebody once that lingers in a place, that houses absorb emotion so it can't get out, and that sometimes, at certain times, in certain places, you can see it, maybe when different times touch in the same place, like when something happens to you and it reminds you a lot of something else, and the two things become associated in your head, he thought ghosts must be like that, people who had lived here, or would live here. This frightened me quite a bit, but Patrick said not to worry, I was safe as long as I respected their territory. And I asked him how I'd know if I'd stepped into their territory or not, and he said I'd know, that I'd be able to feel it at the back of my neck, and a bit in the lower part of my body, a feeling of cold and fear and anticipation, much like—

RUFFING. Much like what?

GILLIAN. Much like what a person feels when they desire another person. It makes the body tremble.

RUFFING. And you didn't think it was highly improper for a servant to be speaking to you in this way?

GILLIAN. Patrick was my friend, and we were speaking true things about something we cared about. There is never any shame in speaking the truth, don't you think? I mean, your job is to investigate the truth, how can you think it's indecent to speak of it?

RUFFING. Did he speak to you often about such things?

GILLIAN. You mean ghosts?

RUFFING. I mean adult matters.

GILLIAN. Inspector, have I been shocking you? If I have, then you're easily shocked, and I don't think that's true, so you must be only pretending to be a little shocked, but not too shocked, because that's what police inspectors are supposed to be like. Only you're not, you're actually fairly cynical about such things, except probably in the case of your daughter. Have you never spoken to your daughter about adult matters?

RUFFING. My daughter has nothing to do with this.

GILLIAN. I think she does, because you have something to do with this, and she has a great deal to do with you, so we have guilt by association.

RUFFING. I'm not guilty of anything.

GILLIAN. Oh, you must be guilty of something. It's just a question of what. Look at you, you're a very smart fellow, you wouldn't have been sent way out here in the middle of nowhere unless you'd done something terribly wrong. I mean, really, you're smart enough to be running something in London, you should be in your prime, and instead they've stuck you out here in the country. Whatever you did, it wasn't bad enough to get you fired, but it must have been serious, because you're very good. Do you have a drinking problem? Or was it some woman? My guess is, both, starting about the time your wife died. Am I wrong?

RUFFING. (*Looks at her. Long pause.*) So Patrick was wrong about the ghosts being harmless. Clearly they weren't harmless if they killed him.

GILLIAN. You're not going to be my friend any more, are you?

RUFFING. Just answer the question.

GILLIAN. You told me something about your personal life because you thought it would loosen me up, so you could get information out of me, but I used it instead to embarrass you and put you off, so now you're closing up in the shell of authority and you don't like me any more. Of course, you didn't like me in the first place, you were just trying to use my weakness to your advantage, and now that I've done the same to you, you're angry at me.

RUFFING. Gillian, there are things more important than your personal feelings or mine.

GILLIAN. What could be more important than what people feel?

RUFFING. What happened.

GILLIAN. But they're the same thing.

RUFFING. What happened is what happened, regardless of how you or I feel about it.

GILLIAN. What happened happened because somebody felt something and also you don't know what happened and what you finally decide happened will have as much to do with how you feel as it does with what happened. What happened has everything in the world to do with how we feel.

RUFFING. You know something you're not telling me, and if you don't stop playing games and answering questions with fairy tales and conundrums you're going to be in a lot of trouble.

GILLIAN. Now you're threatening me. You're trying to alter reality with threats. It's just the other side of praying. And every bit as useless.

RUFFING. Will you please just answer the question?

GILLIAN. I've forgotten what it was.

RUFFING. How can the ghosts be harmless if they killed Patrick?

GILLIAN. Maybe he accidentally invaded their territory in some way, and then couldn't get away. You can't blame the ghosts for that. That would be a kind of accident, wouldn't it? If he'd just gotten in their way? I mean, ghosts must be very obsessed with what they're doing, what they're re-enacting, don't you think? They're like actors at a rehearsal of something that's already happened, or is doomed to happen, that's the script, and they've got to keep going over and over it again and again until they get it right, but they can't get it right, because it's already happened wrong, or will happen wrong, do you see? Purgatory is a bad rehearsal.

RUFFING. Then if someone else stumbles into their territory again, that person could be murdered, too. Does that follow?

GILLIAN. It seems to me a distinct possibility.

RUFFING. Tell me about Patrick and Marcy.

GILLIAN. What about them?

RUFFING. They were special friends, weren't they?

GILLIAN. Why would you think that?

RUFFING. Did you ever see Patrick in Marcy's room?

GILLIAN. No. Well, actually, yes.

RUFFING. Often?

GILLIAN. Once. And I didn't see him, I only heard him. They were having an argument.

RUFFING. When was this? Recently?

GILLIAN. Not too long ago.

RUFFING. What were they arguing about?

GILLIAN. I don't know.

RUFFING. You heard them arguing, you must have heard some words.

GILLIAN. Patrick said something about a child.

RUFFING. A child? What about a child?

GILLIAN. I don't know. That's all I remember. But Marcy was very upset. Extremely. That's unusual, she doesn't get upset, at least she doesn't let it show, not often. You're like her, you know. You'd make a lovely couple, in fact.

RUFFING. Try to remember how recently this was. It's very important.

GILLIAN. It might have been last week.

RUFFING. You're sure you're not making this up?

GILLIAN. Oh, I wouldn't lie to you, John. You're my friend. You mustn't be cross with me. You know I'm only trying to help you find the truth.

(MARCY moves into the light. GILLIAN, smiling, very pleased with herself, moves into the shadows.)

RUFFING. Was Patrick Roarke ever in your room?

MARCY. No.

RUFFING. Never?

MARCY. Not that I recall.

RUFFING. Gillian says she heard Patrick arguing with you in your room a week before his death.

MARCY. She's mistaken.

RUFFING. Why would she make that up?

MARCY. I didn't say she made it up, I said she was mistaken.

RUFFING. You never had an argument with Patrick?

MARCY. Not in my room

RUFFING. But you did argue with him?

MARCY. I might have.

RUFFING. About what?

MARCY. I don't remember.

RUFFING. Was it about a child?

MARCY. What child?

RUFFING. Gillian said the argument was about a child.

MARCY. Inspector, this is the girl who's been trying to convince you a ghost killed Patrick, and you believe her when she tells you a story about some child?

RUFFING. At this point I'm not sure what to believe.

MARCY. That's your problem, not mine.

RUFFING. No, it's your problem, because what I report will determine whether or not someone is charged and brought to trial, and what the charge will be, and right now everything points directly at you.

MARCY. Oh, believe what you like. You will anyway. Nothing I say means anything to you.

RUFFING. You don't help yourself by being rude.

MARCY. Neither do you.

RUFFING. Something is going on in this house, and if you know what it is, believe me, you're much better off telling me here and now than you will be if I find out later that you've been misleading me in any way. Now, are you going to help me or not?

(SHE looks away from him. Silence.)

RUFFING. All right then. But God help you if I find out I've been lied to. (*HE moves angrily away from her.*)

MARCY. Inspector?

RUFFING. Yes? What is it?

MARCY. Have you questioned Mrs. French yet?

RUFFING. No. Why?

MARCY. I think you should.

RUFFING. Why?

MARCY. I just think you should. Excuse me.

(SHE moves into the shadows. MRS. FRENCH moves into the light.)

RUFFING. How long have you been housekeeper here?

MRS. FRENCH. I was housemaid for Mr. Ravenscroft's parents when I was a girl. I grew up in this house.

RUFFING. How long have you known Mrs. Ravenscroft?

MRS. FRENCH. Since Mr. Ravenscroft brought her from London, eighteen or nineteen years ago.

RUFFING. Where were you when Patrick died?

MRS. FRENCH. In bed. I heard Mrs. Ravenscroft calling me and got up to see what was the matter. My room is back of the kitchen. I went into the front hallway, and there was Patrick at the foot of the steps, just like—

RUFFING. Just like Mr. Ravenscroft?

MRS. FRENCH. I thought at first it was a bad dream, it happening again that way, I just couldn't believe it.

RUFFING. Where was Mrs. Ravenscroft?

MRS. FRENCH. Standing over him, at the foot of the stairs.

RUFFING. What did she say to you?

MRS. FRENCH. She told me to get Dolly to fetch the doctor, and when I'd done that, I stayed with the body and she went up the steps to Miss Gillian, who was very upset.

RUFFING. Where was Marcy during all this?

MRS. FRENCH. At the top of the steps, looking down. She tried to keep Gillian from seeing, and took her back to her room.

RUFFING. Did you ask Mrs. Ravenscroft what had happened?

MRS. FRENCH. No sir. It seemed pretty obvious what happened.

RUFFING. And what's that?

MRS. FRENCH. That he'd fell down the steps and broke his neck.

RUFFING. When did you first hear that Patrick had been pushed down the steps by Marcy?

MRS. FRENCH. Uh—Dolly told me.

RUFFING. When was this?

MRS. FRENCH. I don't know. Some time that night.

RUFFING. You're certain it was Dolly who told you?

MRS. FRENCH. Why? Is that important?

RUFFING. How did Dolly know?

MRS. FRENCH. She didn't say.

RUFFING. Didn't you ask her how she knew?

MRS. FRENCH. I don't remember. I don't understand what difference it makes. Marcy admitted she pushed him, didn't she?

RUFFING. Do you believe it happened the way she said?

MRS. FRENCH. I'd rather not comment on that.

RUFFING. Does that mean you have some reason not to believe her?

MRS. FRENCH. Nothing it's really my place to talk about.

RUFFING. Mrs. French, you're going to have to talk about it some time, if not now, then in court.

MRS. FRENCH. It's nothing I could prove. It's just that—I don't trust Miss Kleiner.

RUFFING. Why not?

MRS. FRENCH. For one thing, I don't like foreigners.

RUFFING. And?

MRS. FRENCH. And I think she was leading him on.

RUFFING. My impression of Patrick is that he was quite a ladies' man.

MRS. FRENCH. He was a good boy. He wouldn't hurt nobody. He was the handsomest, kindest, cheerfulest young man there ever was, and it was a shame what that foreign hussy did to him, leading him on like that, teasing him.

RUFFING. How did she tease him?

MRS. FRENCH. She'd brush by him in the doorway when there was plenty of room to get through. She'd come to the top of the stairs at night in her nightgown and look down at him, with a good bit of flesh exposed. She teased him, she led him to have hopes, she was cruel to him, then she'd get him hoping again. She played with him, tortured him—

RUFFING. And then killed him?

MRS. FRENCH. I didn't say that.

RUFFING. Do you believe Patrick might have attacked her that night?

MRS. FRENCH. Patrick would never have hurt nobody.

RUFFING. But he was drinking.

MRS. FRENCH. Yes, he drank, he was terribly unhappy about her, he had an infatuation with her, and she took an evil pleasure in it, she drove him nearly insane.

RUFFING. But not insane enough to attack her?

MRS. FRENCH. Crazy enough, maybe, if he'd been drinking, to go up that staircase at night and try to see her.

RUFFING. So you think her story is only part of the truth?

MRS. FRENCH. I would not accuse nobody of murder. Maybe it was an accident, I didn't see it. And to be fair, I can think of no reason why she'd want to kill him. It would spoil all her fun, wouldn't it?

RUFFING. Do you know if he was ever in her room?

MRS. FRENCH. I wouldn't be surprised. Sometimes a woman will tease a man when she doesn't intend to ever give him what he wants, and if the man's been drinking, and is young and strong like Patrick, perhaps a woman might get in over her head, and be frightened, and try to get away, and if he caught her she might push him away from her, and if they happened to be at the top of the staircase, he might fall. But there was provocation. He wouldn't just assault a woman. It ain't right he should bear all the blame. I don't say she planned to kill him. I do say she's the one responsible for him being up there in the first place where he had no business being, and where he was afraid to be.

RUFFING. Afraid?

MRS. FRENCH. Patrick had some foolish idea there was ghosts up there, a silly thing for a big, strong lad like him to be worried about. He always took pride in his courage, he was afraid of no man alive, but he was scared of the top of them steps. Isn't it a queer thing, that it should happen to be the place he'd die?

RUFFING. Did Patrick ever speak to you about a child?

MRS. FRENCH. What child?

RUFFING. Any particular child, especially in relation to Marcy?

MRS. FRENCH. Not that I remember. Is that all? I'm very busy here, that idiot girl has burned most of the dinner.

RUFFING. Actually, it's Dolly I need to speak to now.

MRS. FRENCH. Oh, you don't want to see her, Inspector, you'll be wasting your time if you do, she's the silliest creature God ever made.

RUFFING. Nevertheless, I want to talk to her. Now.

MRS. FRENCH. Whatever you say. DOLLY.

*(DOLLY moves into the light. MRS. FRENCH exchanges
a stern look with her and moves into the shadows.
DOLLY looks at Ruffing and squirms.)*

RUFFING. Don't be afraid, Dolly, I just want to ask
you a couple of questions.

DOLLY. Yes sir.

RUFFING. What happened the night Patrick died?

DOLLY. I heard a commotion and I come out of my
room and Mrs. French was at the foot of the staircase, and
Patrick was layin there like a broken doll. Mrs. French said
run and get the doctor, so I put on my coat and went.

RUFFING. How did you get there?

DOLLY. I rode old Ben. He's one of Mr. Ravenscroft's
horses.

RUFFING. But there was no one to saddle him for you,
with Patrick dead, was there?

DOLLY. I rode him bareback, sir. I'm a country girl,
and a good rider, Patrick took me riding all the time. I
could have put on my own saddle, but there wasn't time,
and I like it better without. I can ride as well as a man.

RUFFING. And when you returned with the doctor, was
Mrs. French still there with the body?

DOLLY. Yes.

RUFFING. Did you see anybody else before you left?

DOLLY. No, sir, just Mrs. French. I believe I heard the
others upstairs, I think Miss Gillian was crying and
screaming some, but I didn't see them.

RUFFING. You're sure? You're absolutely positive?

DOLLY. Yes sir.

RUFFING. That's odd. That's very odd.

DOLLY. What is?

RUFFING. And then what happened?

DOLLY. The doctor looked at Patrick and said he was dead. Well, I could have told you that. It didn't take a blooming genius to see that a man with his head bent near backwards and a blue face was dead. God, it was awful.

RUFFING. Did Mrs. French tell you anything about what happened when she sent you for the doctor?

DOLLY. No, she just said to go fetch him, and when I just sort of stood there, looking at poor Patrick, she slapped me in the face and said to go, and so I went.

RUFFING. She slapped you?

DOLLY. Yes sir.

RUFFING. Does she hit you often?

DOLLY. She was upset.

RUFFING. How long were you gone?

DOLLY. Half an hour, maybe.

RUFFING. When did you tell Mrs. French that Marcy pushed Patrick down the stairs?

DOLLY. Pardon?

RUFFING. Mrs. French says you're the one who told her what happened.

DOLLY. Mrs. French said that?

RUFFING. Yes. Is she wrong?

DOLLY. Um. Well, no sir, I guess if she says so, it must have been me that told her.

RUFFING. And how did you know?

DOLLY. How did I know?

RUFFING. Yes, how did you know that's what happened, if Mrs. French didn't tell you, and you didn't see the other three women at the time, how could you have told her that?

DOLLY. I don't know, sir.

RUFFING. When did you learn that Marcy pushed Patrick down the steps? Who told you that?

DOLLY. It must have been Mrs. French.

RUFFING. But Mrs. French says you told HER. Now, which is it?

DOLLY. I don't know, what does it matter?

RUFFING. It matters because you people are lying to me, every single woman in this house has been lying to me, and I want to know why, and you're going to tell me, Dolly, and you're going to tell me right now.

DOLLY. I don't feel very good, sir, can I be excused?

RUFFING. No, you can't be excused, you're going to tell me the truth, right now, or you're going to be in very serious trouble.

DOLLY. I didn't do nothing, sir, I was just following orders.

RUFFING. Orders from whom? Who told you to lie to me?

DOLLY. Nobody.

RUFFING. Then why did you say you were following orders?

DOLLY. I've got to go, sir. I'm going to throw up, and if I puke here in the study, they'll kill me.

RUFFING. (*Stopping her.*) You're not going anywhere until you tell me the truth. Now, tell me, or I'm going to see to it that you spend the night in jail.

DOLLY. I don't want to go to jail.

RUFFING. Then tell me the truth.

DOLLY. I didn't do nothing.

RUFFING. You're obstructing justice.

DOLLY. Don't hit me.

RUFFING. I'm not going to hit you, dammit, now tell me.

DOLLY. I didn't mean to lie. Mrs. French just said Marcy pushed Patrick down the stairs, and if anybody asked me, that's all I know.

RUFFING. Then Mrs. French lied to me.

DOLLY. I don't know. I'm going to vomit.

RUFFING. But why would she lie to me about that?

DOLLY. I don't know, sir, I don't know nothing about it, I swear, I just do what I'm told, and I burned the gravy and dropped the meat in the sink and the cat ate the pudding and I don't want to lose my job, I got no place to go, I'm a poor orphan girl, why do you want to do this to me? I'm going to spew up breakfast and lunch combined.

RUFFING. Oh, all right, go on, then.

(SHE runs sobbing into the shadows past MRS. FRENCH, who moves into the light.)

MRS. FRENCH. What on earth have you been doing to that girl? She's vomiting in the aspidistra.

RUFFING. Why did you lie to me?

MRS. FRENCH. I beg your pardon?

RUFFING. Dolly didn't tell you Marcy pushed Patrick down the steps.

MRS. FRENCH. Didn't she?

RUFFING. She says you told HER.

MRS. FRENCH. Well, she's such a foolish thing, Inspector, I'm not sure she knows what she told me.

RUFFING. She couldn't have told you. You were there at the body before she was, and she had no chance to speak with the others before the doctor arrived, therefore either

someone else told you what happened, or you saw it
yourself, or you simply made it up.

MRS. FRENCH. Why would I make up a terrible thing
like that?

RUFFING. Then who told you Marcy pushed Patrick
down the stairs?

*(MRS. FRENCH hesitates. MRS. RAVENSCROFT
moves into the light.)*

MRS. RAVENSCROFT. I did.

MRS. FRENCH. Mrs. Ravenscroft, I'm sorry, I—

MRS. RAVENSCROFT. That's all right, Ellen. It's
not your fault. Go away now and let me speak with
Inspector Ruffing.

MRS. FRENCH. Yes mum. *(SHE goes into the
shadows.)*

MRS. RAVENSCROFT. You're considerably sharper
than what they usually send out this way, you know,
Inspector.

RUFFING. Don't flatter me, just tell me what's going
on here.

MRS. RAVENSCROFT. It's nothing so terrible. I told
Mrs. French before I left Patrick's body and went up the
stairs that Marcy had pushed him down the steps.

RUFFING. Then why didn't she just tell me that?

MRS. RAVENSCROFT. She was trying to protect
me.

RUFFING. From what?

MRS. RAVENSCROFT. It's rather complicated.

RUFFING. I'm listening.

MRS. RAVENSCROFT. Inspector, may I speak to you in confidence?

RUFFING. No.

(Pause.)

MRS. RAVENSCROFT. (*Looks at him, sighs.*) Patrick Roarke and I were—somewhat involved. Don't stand there looking like you've just eaten the canary. The thing is, earlier in the evening, Mrs. French walked in on Patrick and me having a quarrel. He'd been drinking. He did have a bit of Irish temper when he'd been drinking.

RUFFING. Was this the first she knew of your relationship with him?

MRS. RAVENSCROFT. Well, if she hadn't suspected before, she certainly knew then, for she found us in a state of—some undress, and well, anyway, when I found Patrick at the foot of the steps I knew Mrs. French might very well jump to the wrong conclusion, so I told her it was Marcy who'd pushed him, and I suppose when you asked her how she knew that, her first thought was to keep me out of it entirely, so she said Dolly had told her. It was a very stupid lie, but her intentions were good, she meant no harm.

RUFFING. But why didn't she just tell me you'd told her?

MRS. RAVENSCROFT. Because she didn't believe me.

RUFFING. She thought you were lying? Surely not just because of one quarrel, even in a state of undress.

MRS. RAVENSCROFT. It's not just that. It's also what happened with my husband.

RUFFING. Your husband? What about your husband?

MRS. RAVENSCROFT. You see, the thing is, my husband did fall down the steps while drunk and break his neck, that part is true, but he was not alone at the time. He was quarrelling with me—he had in fact just thrown me across the hallway and into the wall, and as he stepped back, he fell down the steps. We didn't tell Inspector McCullough or Doctor Witherspoon that because it didn't seem to matter, I mean, my husband was dead, it was clearly an accident. Why circulate more scandal? But when Mrs. French saw that much the same thing had happened to Patrick, I suppose her first assumption, after the somewhat lurid scene she'd witnessed earlier in the evening, was that I must have taken up throwing men down staircases as a kind of hobby or something, and that's why she told you that apparently inconsequential lie, that to a man less rigorous in his attention to detail would have gone quite unremarked and saved me the considerable embarrassment of having this extremely distasteful conversation with you.

RUFFING. So what we have now is two murders.

MRS. RAVENSCROFT. No, what we have is two horrible accidents, two terrible things that happened, an unfortunate coincidence. Have you never been trapped in an unlikely chain of events, and known that no one would possibly believe the truth, that the very act of trying to explain it to anyone would make you appear guilty of something? I think the world quite often does that to people, traps them in outrageous coincidences that make a conclusion appear obvious which in fact is not true.

RUFFING. The truth is that the women in this house have lied about two successive deaths.

MRS. RAVENSCROFT. No one meant any harm, it's just an ugly and messy set of coincidences that got out of hand. If it's anyone's fault, it's mine, don't blame the others.

RUFFING. Then how did Patrick Roarke die?

MRS. RAVENSCROFT. I presume that Marcy pushed him down the stairs, exactly as she told you, and as she told me, when I came out to see what happened.

RUFFING. But the first time I questioned you, you told me she said nothing to you until after you'd gone downstairs, examined the body, spoken to Mrs. French, gone back up to Gillian's room and then come out again.

MRS. RAVENSCROFT. Did I say that? I must have been mistaken.

RUFFING. Or perhaps you and Marcy cooked up the whole story to protect you. Perhaps Mrs. French's suspicions were perfectly justified. Perhaps you did push Patrick down the steps, just as you pushed your husband.

MRS. RAVENSCROFT. No, that isn't true, I wasn't even there, I was in my room, I swear, it happened the way I said.

RUFFING. The way you said which time?

MRS. RAVENSCROFT. The first time. No, I mean the second time.

RUFFING. Perhaps your husband discovered your relationship with Patrick, and that's why you pushed him down the stairs.

MRS. RAVENSCROFT. I didn't push my husband down the stairs. I didn't get involved with Patrick until after my husband's death. I was desperately lonely. I realized soon enough that it was an impossible situation, and I told Patrick so.

RUFFING. The night he died?

MRS. RAVENSCROFT. Yes. That was the quarrel Mrs. French walked in on. I told Patrick we must stop immediately, and never speak of what had happened between us again. He was hurt, he was angry, he was still just a boy in many ways, in his mind, and he was drinking. No doubt he attacked Marcy as some sort of revenge upon me, or out of despair, I don't know, but I'm sure the girl has done nothing wrong, it was just a horrible accident, and it seemed far too private and sordid to try and explain to somebody like you. It was something that just had to do with the people in this house. I don't want that poor girl to suffer for my weakness, but the truth does seem to be that she pushed him down the steps. It doesn't have to come out in public, I hope. I'm thinking of my daughter, of what a scandal like that would do to her.

RUFFING. You might have thought of that before you began carrying on with the footman.

MRS. RAVENSCROFT. Yes, that's it, get high and mighty with me, you be the judge and jury, tell me how evil I am for being lonely and taking what comfort I could find. When a woman does it, it's a crime, but a man can do anything he damned well pleases, like my husband.

RUFFING. Your husband? Was your husband betraying you?

MRS. RAVENSCROFT. Oh, what does it matter?

RUFFING. Who was your husband betraying you with?

MRS. RAVENSCROFT. I have no idea.

RUFFING. Will you stop lying to me?

MRS. RAVENSCROFT. I'm not lying now.

RUFFING. And just how am I supposed to know that?

MRS. RAVENSCROFT. I don't know, that's your job, isn't it?

RUFFING. Now you listen to me. Your only hope is to tell me the absolute truth, from this moment on. If you lie to me again, about anything, large or small, I will have no mercy on you.

MRS. RAVENSCROFT. Does that mean you might have some mercy on me if I tell the truth?

RUFFING. I make no promises.

MRS. RAVENSCROFT. But you do have a great deal of discretion in these matters, don't you? I mean, it's largely up to you to decide if there's anything further to investigate here, so you could help if you wanted to.

RUFFING. I'm not here to help you, I'm here to find the truth.

DOLLY. (*Moving timidly into the light.*) Excuse me, mum, but supper's ready.

MRS. RAVENSCROFT. I don't want any goddamned supper, you stupid little twit, will you just get out of here?

DOLLY. (*Bursting into tears.*) I'm sorry, mum. Mrs. French said—

MRS. RAVENSCROFT. I don't give a good flying vault at the moon what Mrs. French said, Mrs. French is a dirty-minded ignoramus, now, get out.

DOLLY. Yes, mum. (*SHE looks at the Inspector, holds her mouth and runs back into the shadows.*)

RUFFING. That was a bit harsh, wasn't it?

MRS. RAVENSCROFT. If you must know, the truth is that my husband wanted a divorce, and I refused to give him one, for Gillian's sake. It would have killed her. Her health has never been good. That's what my husband and I were quarrelling about the night he died. But it happened exactly as I told you. And apparently because of my own weakness and loneliness afterwards, I was inadvertently the cause of something very similar happening between Marcy and poor Patrick. It's a very sad thing, really, but there was no murder here. I swear, on my honor.

GILLIAN. (*Screaming, from in the shadows.*) NOOOOO. NOOOOOOOOOOOOO.

MRS. RAVENSCROFT. Good God. What is it now? Gillian? Gillian?

GILLIAN. (*Moving into the light.*) I saw it. I saw it again.

RUFFING. What did you see?

GILLIAN. (*As one by one DOLLY, MRS. FRENCH and MARCY move back into the light and look at her.*) — At the top of the steps. I saw the ghost. I saw her. It was a woman, dressed in white, so beautiful, and someone else, darker, a man, I think, just like before. I saw it just before Father died. And I saw it just before Patrick died. Now I've seen it again. (*SHE looks at Ruffing.*) I do hope you've decided to stay for supper after all, Inspector. Perhaps we can have you for dessert.

(*All the WOMEN look at Ruffing. Ticking CLOCK. The LIGHTS fade and go out. End of Act I.*)

ACT II

(Ticking CLOCKS. LIGHTS up on RUFFING, looking out the invisible downstage window, drink in hand. The WOMEN sit in the shadows, as before. MARCY steps into the light.)

MARCY. She's all right. Her mother's with her. It's just the strain of all this, it's been horrible for her. God, look at the snow coming down. It's like being trapped in a house at the end of the world.

RUFFING. It must have been difficult for you to adjust to the isolation out here. Very different from Vienna, isn't it?

MARCY. Isolation is something one carries around with one from place to place.

RUFFING. *(Looking at her.)* You're lonely.

MARCY. So how does that distinguish me from any other person in England? You, for instance.

RUFFING. What makes you think I'm lonely?

MARCY. It's written on your face.

RUFFING. There is nothing written on my face. I'm a police inspector. That's against the rules.

MARCY. And you, of course, always obey the rules.

RUFFING. I do the best I can.

MARCY. Do you like the wine? I see you've had quite a bit.

RUFFING. The wine is very good, yes.

MARCY. I've poisoned it, you know.

57

RUFFING. Pardon?

MARCY. I poisoned your wine. Can't you smell the bitter almond?

RUFFING. (*Looking at the wine, then at her.*) You're joking.

MARCY. Oh, I would never dare to do that, to joke with the great Inspector Ruffing, the great sleuth of the nether reaches of nowhere, the great seeker after truth.

RUFFING. Do you find me that pompous?

MARCY. No, you're not pompous, exactly. You're naive.

RUFFING. Naive?

MARCY. Very.

RUFFING. Well, that's one of the few things I haven't been accused of being. Rude now and then, stubborn. But I'm hardly naive.

MARCY. Anybody that sure of himself must be either naive or just stupid, and I don't think you're stupid.

RUFFING. Well, thank you for the compliment, if that's what it is, but I'm not all that sure of myself. Although there is more than a little benefit to appearing that way, in my profession. You could save us both a lot of trouble, you know, if you'd just tell me what really happened.

MARCY. Do you want to save trouble, or do you want to find the truth? Because sometimes, you know, it's so much trouble finding the truth, you're better off just to settle for the most acceptable agreed upon fabrication.

RUFFING. I can't do that.

MARCY. Of course you can do it. You probably do it all the time. You just don't like to admit it. The fantasy that you don't do it is your most fundamental mutually agreed upon fabrication.

RUFFING. When Mrs. Ravenscroft came out of her room and saw you standing at the top of the stairs, did she say anything to you?

MARCY. She asked me what on earth was going on.

RUFFING. And what did you reply?

MARCY. I don't remember.

RUFFING. Did you tell her you'd pushed Patrick down the stairs?

MARCY. I don't know. I'm not trying to hide anything from you, I was just—rather in shock.

RUFFING. Then she went down the steps to the body—

MARCY. Yes.

RUFFING. And then Gillian came out of her room?

MARCY. Yes.

RUFFING. And what did Gillian say?

MARCY. I don't know. She was upset. She saw Patrick. I tried to keep her away. I took her to her room. I've told you this.

RUFFING. Did you see Mrs. French?

MARCY. I don't remember.

RUFFING. Did you see Dolly?

MARCY. What difference does it make?

RUFFING. The stories don't match, the chronology's off. Mrs. Ravenscroft says she didn't go back upstairs until after Dolly'd been sent for the doctor, but Dolly insists she saw no one but Mrs. French. Somebody is lying.

MARCY. People remember things differently.

RUFFING. No. It's like a gigantic puzzle of which I've got some of the right pieces and some of the wrong ones, but I don't know which is which. It's a mixture of truths, half-truths, hallucinations and half-baked lies stuck together hurriedly by terrified people for reasons which I don't yet comprehend.

MARCY. All I remember is that Mrs. Ravenscroft came back upstairs and she and I got Gillian calmed down in her room, gave her a sedative, and then Mrs. Ravenscroft and I went into my room and I explained to her what had happened, and then the doctor arrived, and that's all. You'd better go easy on that wine. It has a tendency to sneak up on you.

RUFFING. Did you know that Patrick was having an affair with Mrs. Ravenscroft?

MARCY. With Mrs. Ravenscroft?

RUFFING. Does that surprise you?

MARCY. No, that couldn't be true.

RUFFING. Why not?

MARCY. Because it—just couldn't. You've made it up to trick me, haven't you? You're trying to get some sort of reaction from me. Who told you that?

RUFFING. Mrs. Ravenscroft did. Ask her if you like. What's the matter? I thought you had no feelings for Patrick. You seem upset.

MARCY. I'm just surprised.

RUFFING. Why? A ladies man like Patrick, a very attractive young widow, and you apparently would have nothing to do with him. It seems to me quite natural for a man like that to go elsewhere for his needs. Did you think he'd wait around for you forever? Or did you perhaps find out that he was sleeping with the lady of the house, and kill him in a jealous rage?

MARCY. If that were true then why would I be surprised?

RUFFING. You're surprised I found out, and you're terrified you'll be prosecuted for murder.

MARCY. I've told you I pushed him and I've told you it was an accident. If they want to bring me to trial, let them.

RUFFING. There is something not right here, and it isn't ghosts, it's people, it's something that people who live in this house did.

MARCY. Do you have any real evidence for that, or is it just your instinct talking?

RUFFING. Instinct is simply knowledge that's been absorbed by the senses but not yet sorted out by the rational part of one's brain. And, in any case, I have more than instinct to go on. For one thing, I have this letter. (*HE holds up a letter.*)

MARCY. What letter is that?

RUFFING. While you were all occupied with Gillian, I took the opportunity to have a look around here in Mr Ravenscroft's library, and I found this very interesting letter in his desk. It's about you.

MARCY. Is it?

RUFFING. It seems that in Vienna, you were governess for a family named Klippstein, is that right?

MARCY. What about it?

RUFFING. And they had two children, a boy and a girl.

MARCY. Yes.

RUFFING. And the little boy died.

MARCY. He drowned. But not when I was employed by them. It happened after I left.

RUFFING. Why were you dismissed?

MARCY. I wasn't dismissed. I left.

RUFFING. Why?

MARCY. For personal reasons.

RUFFING. Personal reasons involving the man of the house?

MARCY. If it's in the letter, why bother to ask?

RUFFING. I want to hear it from you.

MARCY. I left because Herr Klippstein made indecent advances towards me.

RUFFING. And you gave in to those advances?

MARCY. Eventually I did, yes. Then I left.

RUFFING. And had a child.

MARCY. Yes. I had a child.

RUFFING. Where is this child now?

MARCY. She's being raised at the convent where I stayed.

RUFFING. Then what are you doing in England?

MARCY. I'm earning the money for my child's room and board and her education.

RUFFING. Why would you consent to go so far away from your child? Don't you want to see her?

MARCY. Of course I want to see her. When's the last time you saw YOUR child?

RUFFING. My child is grown.

MARCY. Your child is seventeen and needs you very much.

RUFFING. What the hell do you know about it?

MARCY. Gillian told me.

RUFFING. Gillian is a pathological liar.

MARCY. You're upset. I've touched a nerve. The great Inspector Ruffing is not used to having light shed on his own personal life. How does it feel, Inspector?

RUFFING. My God, I must be slipping. Rule number one is never bring your personal life into an investigation. And rule number two is never tell a woman anything, or as sure as day and night she'll find a way to use it against you.

MARCY. My goodness, we sound bitter. Are we a bitter police inspector?

RUFFING. We are not discussing my relationship with my daughter. We are discussing why you have abandoned yours.

MARCY. I haven't abandoned her. I couldn't find work in Vienna or anywhere near there. Herr Klippstein was not about to give me references, and I couldn't very well bother them, after the death of their son. Oh, why am I trying to explain this to you? You don't care. You just want to prove I'm some sort of scarlet woman who murders people. Well, yes, I was molested by my employer when I was a very young girl, and I had a child whom I love desperately and miss desperately every moment of every day of my life in this wretched, dismal, stuffy, ridiculous, hatefully damp and drafty country. You can accuse me of what you like, but don't tell me I don't love my child. If it weren't for my child I'd have cut my own throat years ago. I'd do anything for her. I'd die for her.

RUFFING. Would you kill for her?

MARCY. In the right circumstances, yes. Wouldn't you? (*SHE is crying softly, trying to hide it.*) Why don't you arrest me and get it over with? Just stop tormenting me.

RUFFING. (*Looking at her, not happy.*) I'm sorry.

MARCY. You're sorry you think I'm a murderer?

RUFFING. I'm sorry I've made you cry.

MARCY. Now you've broken rule number three—never apologize. You're really botching this case up horribly, Inspector.

RUFFING. So Mr. Ravenscroft knew about your child when he hired you?

MARCY. Yes, he knew about all of that.

RUFFING. Did Mrs. Ravenscroft know as well?

MARCY. I doubt that he would have told her. Mrs. Ravenscroft is not as tolerant of human frailties as her husband was.

RUFFING. You believe he concealed these things from her when he hired you?

MARCY. He was a kind man who was trying to help me. He probably saw no reason to upset his wife with that particular information. He knew she wouldn't understand.

RUFFING. Do you really think kindness was his only motive?

MARCY. He needed a companion and governess for Gillian. I needed a position. What other reason could there be?

RUFFING. You know perfectly well what other reason. You're a tremendously attractive woman. Do you expect me to believe that had nothing to do with it?

MARCY. Mr. Ravenscroft had no way of knowing what I looked like, unless the Mother Superior told him, and I rather doubt that. I am, however, flattered to know you find me so tremendously attractive. Watch out, or you'll be breaking yet another rule.

RUFFING. Did anyone else here know about your child?

MARCY. I don't think so.

RUFFING. That's a lie. Patrick knew. That's the child Gillian heard you arguing about in your room.

MARCY. All right, yes, Patrick knew. I expect he was snooping about in Mr. Ravenscroft's papers after he died. Patrick was curious as a cat, he was a gossip, and he loved to know things so he could tease people about them, and get favors from them for not telling.

RUFFING. In other words, Patrick was blackmailing you. He found this letter and threatened to tell Mrs. Ravenscroft what was in it, and so you killed him.

MARCY. That's stupid. You didn't know Patrick, he was not a criminal, he would never blackmail anybody. You think like a policeman, you make everything seem filthy, but the world is infinitely more ambiguous than you want it to be. You keep trying to force everything to conform to your own dumb preconceptions and you only create more lies.

RUFFING. I'm creating lies? Well, that's a good one. What the devil have you people been doing but lying to me every time you open your damned mouths?

MARCY. Patrick was not blackmailing me, he didn't care about money. He was always giving it away.

RUFFING. If not for money, then for love perhaps. For sexual favors. There, at least, is something Patrick clearly did care about. He threatened to show Mrs. Ravenscroft this letter, didn't he?

MARCY. But he never would have done it. I know he wouldn't. And she might just as easily have found it herself.

RUFFING. Not if Patrick had it. He kept it so you'd sleep with him. You hoped he wouldn't show her, but you couldn't know for sure, the world being, as you say, a very ambiguous place, and he was very drunk that night, you didn't know what he'd do, so you lured him out onto the staircase and then pushed him. Perhaps you even thought they'd suspect Mrs. Ravenscroft, after what happened to her husband, and the affair with Patrick.

MARCY. I didn't know about her affair with Patrick. And if Patrick was blackmailing me with the letter, then why would he put it back? You found it in Mr. Ravenscroft's desk, so how did it get there, if Patrick was blackmailing me with it?

RUFFING. But you admitted he'd seen it.

MARCY. Yes, he saw it, and he taunted me with it, but if he was going to blackmail me why on earth would he leave it there for you or Mrs. Ravenscroft to find?

RUFFING. Well, he didn't know I was coming, did he? I mean, he didn't know you were going to murder him. Maybe Mrs. Ravenscroft surprised him reading it, and he had to put it away quickly and never got a chance to retrieve it before you killed him. It's enough that he knew it was there.

MARCY. You see what you're doing? You think you know the answer, so you're trying to twist all the facts to make them conform to your stupid theory. Well, I'm sorry to disappoint you, Inspector, but it happened exactly the way I said.

GILLIAN. (*Moving into the light, in her nightgown.*) What are you shouting at Marcy for?

MARCY. Gillian, you're supposed to be in bed, what are you doing here? You'll catch something.

GILLIAN. You musn't yell at Marcy like that. She hasn't done anything.

MARCY. Gillian, go back to your room, right now.

RUFFING. I'm afraid she has done something, Gillian. She's lied to me, she's concealed evidence, and she very likely killed your friend Patrick to keep him from telling your mother something about her past that would have lost her her job and severely jeopardized the future of someone she loves very much. I'm afraid your friend Marcy is going to prison for a long time. Or worse.

GILLIAN. No. You can't do that. Marcy didn't kill Patrick.

RUFFING. You don't know what she did.

GILLIAN. Yes, I do know.

MARCY. Gillian, for God's sake, shut up and go back to bed.

GILLIAN. They're all trying to protect me, you see. That's what all this desperate prevarication has been about. They're just getting trapped further and further in lie after lie and it isn't going to work, because you're too smart for them, Inspector, so I might just as well tell you the truth and be done with it.

MARCY. Gillian, you don't know what you're saying. Be quiet this instant and go back to your room, or I shall be very cross with you.

GILLIAN. I killed Patrick. I pushed him down the staircase, and it wasn't any accident. I did it on purpose.

MARCY. Inspector, you mustn't believe anything she says, she's not well, really.

RUFFING. But why would you push Patrick down the stairs?

GILLIAN. That's for me to know and you to find out.

RUFFING. Gillian, this is very serious, now, this is a matter of life and death, and you mustn't say things to me that you don't mean, and if you do mean them, you need to understand that anything you say could incriminate you further and be used against you.

GILLIAN I don't care.

MARCY. MRS. RAVENSCROFT—

GILLIAN. I did it. I killed him. It's true. So leave Marcy alone.

MARCY. MRS. RAVENSCROFT. GET IN HERE AT ONCE.

RUFFING. I don't believe you, Gillian. You liked Patrick, he was your friend. You'd never do that to him, would you?

GILLIAN. I did. I swear I did.

MARCY. No she didn't.

GILLIAN. Yes I did.

MRS. RAVENSCROFT (*Moving into the light.*) What is it? Marcy, what are you bellowing about? Inspector, what have you been doing to my child? Why is she in her nightgown?

RUFFING. Your child has just confessed to the murder of Patrick Roarke.

MRS. RAVENSCROFT Oh, that's absurd. Why would she do a thing like that?

RUFFING. She refuses to say.

MRS. RAVENSCROFT Well, that proves she's lying.

RUFFING. Why would your daughter confess to a murder she didn't commit?

MRS. RAVENSCROFT Why does she ever do anything? Do you think her objective is to make sense? I've never understood a thing that child has said or done. She's always been like a creature from some other planet. I can't talk to her. I can't get her to do anything. She lives in a fantasy world. She's really not competent, Inspector, and

I think it should be obvious to you by now that you can't believe a word she says.

RUFFING. Your mother doesn't believe you either, Gillian.

GILLIAN. Yes she does. She knows it's true. Look at her.

RUFFING. Why would she pretend not to believe you?

GILLIAN. Because, stupid, she wants you to think I'm insane, so you won't believe me, either, or at the very least, that I couldn't be held responsible. But the fact is, I'm perfectly sane, and I did do it. I'll swear to it in court. So come on, arrest me, wrap my frail, nubile young trembling body in chains, come on. (*SHE holds out her wrists.*)

RUFFING. I'm not going to believe you until you can give me one good reason why you'd do such a thing to your bosom friend Patrick.

(*GILLIAN looks at him, hesitates, then starts to say something when DOLLY scuttles into the light, flustered and upset.*)

DOLLY. Mrs. French wants to know would anybody like hot chocolate? Now don't start yelling at me because it wasn't my idea but Mrs. French says if everybody is going to be up shouting and screaming at one another all night perhaps somebody would like hot chocolate, and I begged her not to send me in, because I don't like being yelled at all the time, but she made me, so if nobody wants any, I'll just go away. Good night.

GILLIAN. I pushed Patrick down the stairs because I was jealous, because Patrick was sleeping with Dolly.

DOLLY. Pardon?

MRS. RAVENSCROFT. With Dolly?

DOLLY. Pardon?

MRS. RAVENSCROFT. Patrick was sleeping with Dolly?

DOLLY. Who was? It wasn't me, I didn't do anything, I just work here, and nobody wants no hot chocolate so I'm going now.

RUFFING. Stay right there.

GILLIAN. It's true, I was in love with Patrick, and I found out he was sleeping with Dolly, and I was very angry at him, so I pushed him down the stairs.

DOLLY. I want to go home.

MRS. RAVENSCROFT. Oh, shut up, Dolly. You ARE home.

DOLLY. I feel sick. I'm dizzy.

RUFFING. Dolly, listen to me. Gillian has just accused you of sleeping with Patrick. Is she telling the truth or isn't she?

DOLLY. Oh, Miss Ravenscroft is a good girl, Inspector. She'd never lie to a policeman.

RUFFING. Then you admit it?

DOLLY. Admit what?

RUFFING. That you slept with Patrick Roarke?

DOLLY. No sir, never, I swear on my mother's grave.

MRS. RAVENSCROFT. Your mother lives over a pub in Bristol.

DOLLY. I swear on my mother's pub.

RUFFING. Then Gillian is lying.

DOLLY. Oh, no sir.

RUFFING. Well, it can't be both. Which is it?

DOLLY. Which is what?

GILLIAN. Are you calling me a liar, Dolly?

DOLLY. Oh, I'd never do that, Miss, that would be disrespectful. I could lose my job.

RUFFING. Did you sleep with Patrick or didn't you?

DOLLY. I'm going to faint, I'm going to throw up, I'm going to die, I'm shaking all over, I can't stand it, I can't stand it, oh God, I wish I was in France.

MRS. FRENCH. (*Moving into the light.*) What on earth is the matter, girl? Can't you even ask them if they want hot chocolate without having a hysterical fit?

DOLLY. I'm going to die, I'm going to die.

MRS. FRENCH Oh, stop blathering, you nitwit. What's the matter with you?

RUFFING. Gillian says Dolly was sleeping with Patrick.

MRS. FRENCH With her? Patrick slept with her?

GILLIAN. It's true. I saw them in the hayloft. It was a Wednesday. They were completely naked. They were going at it like monkeys.

MRS. RAVENSCROFT. Gillian!

DOLLY. It isn't true, I never, I swear I never, it wasn't me, it was Mrs. French.

MRS. RAVENSCROFT. You slept with Mrs. French?

DOLLY. No, Patrick did.

MRS. FRENCH. What in God's name are you saying, girl?

DOLLY. I'm sorry, I'm sorry, I wish I was dead, I wish God would come in a trolly car and take me to heaven right now, I don't want to live any more, and I'm going to throw up, but it was Mrs. French slept with him, I swear.

MRS. FRENCH. Why, you lying little guttersnipe.

(SHE grabs Dolly by the shoulders and begins shaking her violently back and forth. DOLLY lolls about like a rag doll.)

MRS. FRENCH. Take that back. Take it back, you slut.

DOLLY. AHHHHHHHHHHHH.

RUFFING. Here now, stop that, stop it. (*HE gets between them and puts his arm around Dolly.*)

MRS. FRENCH. That stupid little tart, accusing me God knows what form of indecency, when everybody knows she's the loosest doxy in England.

DOLLY. That's a lie. I never. Well, hardly ever. And not with Patrick. It was you. You did it. I don't want to go to jail, I don't want to go to jail, I'm a poor orphan, I swear, you can ask my mother.

RUFFING. Now just settle down here, everybody, and let's try to make some sense out of all this. Dolly, here, now, child, don't blubber, it's all right, nobody's going to hurt you, come on, you're not accused of any crime, we just need to know the truth. Come on. Settle down. Just tell me the truth, and everything will be all right.

(DOLLY has calmed down considerably with his cuddling and attention, and looks up at him, sniffing.)

RUFFING. That's it. There's a brave girl. So, we're all right now, aren't we?

DOLLY. No.

RUFFING. Yes we are.

DOLLY. Maybe you are. I'm not.

MRS. RAVENSCROFT. Oh, for God's sake, stop babying the little booby. Mrs. French, you have at least some functional brain matter, tell me straight out, did you sleep with Patrick?

MRS. FRENCH. That, madam, is a disgusting question, and one that I consider it beneath you to ask or me to answer.

MRS. RAVENSCROFT. I take it that means yes.

(MRS. FRENCH glares at her.)

RUFFING. Well?

MRS. FRENCH. Whatever happened between Patrick and me has nothing to do with his death.

RUFFING. So. Mrs. French slept with Patrick, according to Dolly, who herself went at it with him in the hayloft like monkeys, according to Gillian, and Mrs. Ravenscroft has admitted to sleeping with Patrick—

DOLLY. Mrs. Ravenscroft? Really?

MRS. RAVENSCROFT. Shut up, Dolly.

GILLIAN. Mother, shame on you.

RUFFING. And Miss Kleiner—

MARCY. Did NOT sleep with Patrick.

RUFFING. Says she didn't sleep with Patrick.

GILLIAN. *(Raising her hand and waving it.)* Me. Me. Don't forget me.

MRS. RAVENSCROFT. Gillian, you did not sleep with Patrick.

GILLIAN. I did too. It was very nice. He told me I was a lot better at it than you were.

MRS. RAVENSCROFT. Gillian—

MARCY. My God.

RUFFING. Well, that appears to explain why Patrick was so dreadfully anxious to get at Marcy, as she seems to have been the only woman in the immediate vicinity whose knickers he had not managed to separate from her person.

MRS. RAVENSCROFT. Inspector, must you be vulgar? How much of that wine have you had?

RUFFING. Clearly not enough. (*HE pours more wine for himself.*)

MRS. RAVENSCROFT. In any case, she's no better than the rest of us, the toast of Vienna, there. We all knew he was sleeping with HER.

MARCY. That's a lie.

GILLIAN. My goodness, Inspector, you're the only one left, if we don't count the horses. You didn't sleep with him, too, did you?

RUFFING. In other words, in all likelihood, Patrick Roarke was bedding down turn and turn about with every woman in this house.

MARCY. Inspector, what's the point of all this, except to satisfy your own lascivious and morbid curiosity? Are you going to arrest anyone or aren't you?

RUFFING. By all rights I should arrest Gillian. She's confessed, and for want of a better explanation, I suppose I have no choice but to presume she's telling the truth.

MRS. RAVENSCROFT. But she's NOT telling the truth.

RUFFING. How do you know?

MRS. RAVENSCROFT. Well, because—because I saw Marcy do it.

MARCY. That isn't true.

MRS. RAVENSCROFT. Yes, I'm afraid it is.

MARCY. You saw no such thing.

MRS. RAVENSCROFT. I'm sorry, I was trying to protect you, dear, I felt so sorry for you, being a foreigner and all, but the truth will out, you might as well confess, it's all for the best, in the end.

MARCY. You shameless, shameless woman. After all I've gone through to protect your daughter—

MRS. RAVENSCROFT. Be quiet about my daughter.

RUFFING. What about her daughter?

DOLLY. Can I go now?

RUFFING, MRS. RAVENSCROFT & MRS. FRENCH. NOOOOO.

DOLLY. But I'm going to puke again.

RUFFING. Well then, go ahead and puke, I don't care, just do NOT leave this room.

DOLLY. I'm going to be so sick. It ain't fair to treat me this way. I'm pregnant.

MRS. FRENCH. You're what?

DOLLY. I'm pregnant. Patrick got me pregnant and then she went and pushed him down the stairs.

RUFFING. Who did? Which she?

DOLLY. Mrs. French.

MRS. FRENCH. You lying little whore.

DOLLY. It's true, she was jealous because Patrick was in love with me, so she killed him, I know she did, she murdered him.

MRS. FRENCH. That does it. (*SHE goes after Dolly again and this time gets her hands around her throat and knocks her to the ground.*)

DOLLY. AHHHHHHHHHHH.

MRS. FRENCH. (*Strangling her.*) You want to see a murder, girl? I'll show you a murder.

DOLLY.   AHHHH. MURDER. MURDER.
AHHHHHHH.

RUFFING. (*Trying to pull her off.*) STOP THAT.
STOP IT.

MRS. RAVENSCROFT. MRS. FRENCH. ELLEN.
ELLEN.

DOLLY.   AHHHHHHHHHHHH. UGGGGGGGG.
UHHHHHHHH.

MRS. FRENCH. BAWD. STRUMPET. HARLOT.

RUFFING. (*Managing finally to pull Mrs. French
away.*) All right, that's enough, that's enough, now
everybody just shut your bloody yaps.

(*THEY all shut up, including DOLLY, still on the floor,
holding her throat, who stops in mid-sobbing gag.*)

MRS. RAVENSCROFT. Inspector, is that any way to
speak to a group of ladies?

RUFFING. Is this any way for a group of ladies to
behave? Running about screaming and denouncing one
another as murderers and trollops and trying to strangle the
maid?

MRS. RAVENSCROFT. Nevertheless, you're a guest
in my house, and there are still proprieties to be observed.
One does not shout at a lady to shut her bloody yap.

RUFFING. You're right, forgive me. Murder and
adultery are one thing, but rudeness is quite another. I think
I'll just have a drink to steady my nerves.

MRS. RAVENSCROFT. You've had too much to
drink already.

RUFFING. On the contrary, I'm just getting started,
but, frankly, I've had just about enough of you, as the boy

said riding the cow, so let's get this thing straight, once and for all. If I don't get the truth from you people immediately so help me God I'm going to run the whole pack of you in on suspicion of murder.

MRS. RAVENSCROFT. You can't do that.

RUFFING. Of course I can do that. I am the voice of authority. I am the dead Queen's left buttock. Rule Britannia.

MRS. RAVENSCROFT. But, Inspector, if you arrest an entire household of women, you'll be the laughingstock of the entire country. You'll probably lose your position.

RUFFING. Oh, my God, what a tragedy that would be. Here I am, with the greatest job a man ever had, out in the middle of god-awful nowhere, in a drafty old house out of a wretched Gothic novel, hopelessly entangled in a moronic ghost and murder mystery too stupid for the theatre, even, I've been banished to this godforsaken snowbound hell-hole, my career can't get any worse, I might as well find the bloody truth and be done with it. Now just what the hell IS the bloody truth? Let us summarize. Patrick was sleeping with Mrs. French, with Miss Ravenscroft, with Mrs. Ravenscroft, and he's got Dolly preggers. At the time of his death he was chasing after the governess in a desperate attempt, one can only presume, to complete a full house, as it were, and he dies the same way his master died three months earlier, by taking a head first plunge down the main staircase, the supposed victim of a ghost in a white dress. Does that about cover it?

MRS. RAVENSCROFT. What a vulgar man you turned out to be, Inspector. You disappoint me greatly.

RUFFING. That's all right, I disappoint myself as well, but that notwithstanding, if nobody is going to step forward and clear this thing up for me, I'll simply have to arrest the most likely candidate. Now, if I arrest Dolly or Mrs. French, no one will care, they're just servants, they're highly expendable. Likewise, Marcy means absolutely nothing to anybody in England, nobody would lift a finger to help any one of them. So I'm left with Mrs. Ravenscroft and her daughter. Of the two, I like Gillian much better, God knows why, but I think the best way to resolve this thing is to arrest her for murder, since everybody else here seems to be trying to protect her, so, all right, Gillian Ravenscroft, I arrest you for the murder of Patrick Roarke.

GILLIAN. Only if I can have handcuffs.

RUFFING. All right. You can have handcuffs.

GILLIAN. Oh, good. Isn't this exciting?

MRS. RAVENSCROFT. You can't put my daughter in handcuffs.

RUFFING. I can if I can only remember where I put the damned things. And why is this room bouncing around like a crate of kangaroos? Is this an earthquake?

MRS. RAVENSCROFT. You're drunk, Inspector. Now take your hands off my daughter this instant or I'll call the police.

RUFFING. I AM the police

MRS. RAVENSCROFT. I'll call other police. Sober police.

RUFFING. Madam, there ARE no sober police. There is no other. The snow surrounds us. I am the only male figure present. Except for the dead. I am the voice of reason and God's representative in the Paradise of Fools, and I arrest your daughter for murder.

MRS. RAVENSCROFT. Inspector, if you do this, I'll have your head on a platter.

RUFFING. You can have my butt in a basket if you'll just tell me who the hell really killed Patrick.

MRS. RAVENSCROFT. All right, then, I did it. Now let her go.

GILLIAN. You didn't kill Patrick, Mama.

MRS. RAVENSCROFT. Yes, I did, so leave my daughter alone. If you must arrest someone, arrest me.

MRS. FRENCH. It wasn't her. It was me. I did it.

GILLIAN. I did it.

RUFFING. Well, now, look here, we can't have everybody jumping up claiming to be Spartacus, now, can we? Why is this so difficult? Sherlock Holmes never had this much trouble. Am I losing my touch? Am I losing my grip? Am I going to puke in the aspidistra?

MRS. RAVENSCROFT. Listen, Inspector. I have a proposition for you. How would you like to retire?

RUFFING. What, and give up show business?

MRS. RAVENSCROFT. I'm lonely, Inspector. I've been a widow three months now, and I can't stand it any more. I must confess that I've taken quite a serious fancy to you. You're good looking, in a rugged, craggy sort of way. You're strong, intelligent, you have a sense of humor, you're dedicated to your work, how would you like to be the new Lord of Ravenscroft manor? I could make it very comfortable here for you. Your daughter would be set for life. You could give up all this messy police work and relax in the bosom of a warm and caring family. Wouldn't you like that? Forgive me for being so forward, but the lips must speak what the heart knows.

RUFFING. You're not trying to bribe me, are you?

MRS. RAVENSCROFT. Bribe? Me? Bribe you? Me bribe you? I would never do a thing like that. I'm shocked that the thought would even cross your mind. The truth is, I've fallen desperately and hopelessly in love with you.

RUFFING. Well. That's flattering. What about you, Mrs. French?

MRS. FRENCH. What about me?

RUFFING. Are you also willing to take me into your bosom? Have you fallen desperately and hopelessly in love with me as well?

MRS. FRENCH. (*Looking at him.*) It's possible.

GILLIAN. And me. Don't forget me. I've been desperately and hopelessly in love with you since the first moment I set eyes upon you, Inspector.

RUFFING. Excellent. Well, that makes three. Dolly? What about you?

DOLLY. Me?

RUFFING. Are you also desperately and hopelessly in love with me?

DOLLY. I just want to crawl under the rug and die.

MRS. RAVENSCROFT. Oh, Dolly, don't be coy. I've seen the way you look at the Inspector. I think you're secretly desperately and hopelessly in love with him, too, aren't you? Dolly? Dolly? Speak up, dear, the Inspector can't hear you. Say it. I am desperately—

DOLLY. I am desperately—

MRS. RAVENSCROFT. —and hopelessly in love with Inspector Ruffing.

DOLLY. Yes. What you said.

RUFFING. This is so touching. I'm deeply moved. But what about Marcy? Are you desperately and hopelessly in love with me as well?

MARCY. Certainly not.

MRS. RAVENSCROFT. Marcy.

RUFFING. No? I've been rejected? Because I don't know that I could be happy unless I had the complete devotion of Patrick's entire harem. I'm afraid it's all or nothing.

MRS. RAVENSCROFT. Marcy. Tell him you love him.

MARCY. I don't love him.

MRS. RAVENSCROFT. Tell him you love him, dammit.

MARCY. How can you do this? How can you all prostitute yourselves to this man like this? And you'd even give him Gillian, your own daughter, a child who's not even in her right mind?

GILLIAN. Hey.

MRS. RAVENSCROFT. Would you rather have her convicted of murder? Or her mother convicted of murder? And what would happen to your own precious child in Vienna, the one you've abandoned, what will her life be like if we all go to prison? Either you go along with this or she gets nothing.

MARCY. I will not be part of this.

RUFFING. Well, then, I have no choice but to arrest Mrs. Ravenscroft for attempting to corrupt a police officer. Come along, sweetheart. (*HE takes her elbow.*)

MRS. RAVENSCROFT. You can't arrest me.

RUFFING. Yes I can. You can look it up. Come along, get your coat, dear, we can't have you catching a chill out there. Pretty nippy this time of night, what?

MRS. RAVENSCROFT. I can't go out there tonight. We'll never get through. The snow's much too high. They'll find me frozen in the morning like Lot's wife.

RUFFING. Oh, we'll make it through, somehow. Where's your faith in the Lord, woman? Pray, speak to God about it. He'll keep you warm. You'll probably wake up in hell.

MRS. RAVENSCROFT. I'm not going out there. I absolutely refuse.

RUFFING. Ah. Resisting arrest. That compounds the offense further, probably add five to ten on your life sentence. Gillian will be a wrinkled old granny before you get out.

GILLIAN. It's all right, Mother. I'll come and see you. Mrs. French can bake you muffins, Marcy will make her famous strudel, and Dolly can bring her baby.

MRS. RAVENSCROFT. I am NOT going to prison. Will you take your hands off me, you drunken oaf?

RUFFING. And I thought you were desperately in love with me. How fickle women are. Maybe I should just get a dog.

MRS. RAVENSCROFT. Let me go. Let me go.

RUFFING. Then tell me the truth, right now, tell me exactly what happened. No more lies, no more half-truths, no more bribery, no more ridiculous attempts to buy me off with flesh, you tell me the truth and the whole truth so help you God right now, or off we go into the snowdrifts, I swear, like Yukon Pete and his Eskimo wife. So? Which is it? Truth or consequences?

(A moment. THEY all look at him.)

RUFFING. No? Nobody? All righty. Off we go. Bundle up, love, we don't want frostbitten titties, do we?

MRS. RAVENSCROFT. I do believe the man's insane. HELP. HELP ME.

(HE is trying to pull her out by the waist, while SHE holds on for dear life to the furniture.)

MRS. RAVENSCROFT. HELP. HELP. HELP ME. SOMEBODY. HELP ME.

(GILLIAN picks up a large old vase and smashes Ruffing violently over the head with it.)

RUFFING. Ahhhhhhhhhhh. *(HE staggers, looks at them, falls to his knees, then onto his face, thud. Pause.)*
MRS. RAVENSCROFT. Oh, my God. What have you done? Gillian, what have you done?
GILLIAN. I just hit him a little whack on the head with that old vase.
MRS. RAVENSCROFT. Gillian, how could you? How could you do such a thing? That vase was worth a fortune. It's been in our family for generations, ever since your great-great-grandfather stole it from the French. Why couldn't you hit him with the poker?
DOLLY. She's killed him. He's dead.
GILLIAN. I didn't mean to. It was an accident. The vase slipped out of my hand and landed on his head. It's a shame, I really did rather fancy him.
DOLLY. We're all going to jail. They're going to hang us from the nearest forest. We're going to die. We're all going to die. I don't want to die. I'm too young. I'm too attractive. My breasts are still getting bigger. Who's going to have my baby for me when I'm dead?

MRS. RAVENSCROFT. Oh, stuff a rag in it, Dolly.

MRS. FRENCH. It's clear what we must do now. We must bury him in the garden, and hope nobody comes for him. We'll just say he never arrived. They'll presume he was caught in the storm, lost his way and froze to death somewhere out there in the snow.

GILLIAN. I don't think we should bury him.

MRS. RAVENSCROFT. Well, we can't just leave him to rot here in the library, dear. Somebody will notice eventually. I suppose we could put him in the closet when the vicar comes, but still, there's the smell to think of.

GILLIAN. Yes, but he moved.

MARCY. (*Examining him.*) He isn't dead. Dolly, run and get some water and a towel. Go on. Go.

(DOLLY scurries into the shadows.)

GILLIAN. I'm so glad he isn't dead. I think I'd like to marry him. Or perhaps have him for a papa. He'd make a nice, cuddly papa, don't you think? Not that my papa wasn't nice.

MRS. RAVENSCROFT. Hush, Gillian.

GILLIAN. My papa was nice sometimes, but other times he was awfully strange.

MRS. RAVENSCROFT. Gillian, be quiet. Go to your room.

MRS. FRENCH. Perhaps we should hit him again.

MARCY. Don't you dare. Get away from him. Give him some air.

DOLLY. (*Running back into the light with a large glass of water.*) Here's the water. (*SHE throws the water in Ruffing's face.*)

MARCY. Dolly, what are you doing?

RUFFING. Ah. Eccccch. Ahhhh.

MARCY. Easy, Inspector. Easy. You're all right.

RUFFING. Am I dead?

MARCY. No, you're not dead, don't be silly.

RUFFING. But I saw them.

MARCY. Saw whom?

RUFFING. On the staircase. I saw them. There was a woman, and she was, it was dark, I tried to kiss her, on the stairs—

MARCY. Just take it easy, Inspector.

RUFFING. What happened?

MARCY. You fell and hit your head.

RUFFING. Fell? On the staircase?

MARCY. No, on the rug. You tripped on the rug.

RUFFING. I don't trip on rugs. I'm an athlete, woman. I played rugby. Damned well, too. Better than those rich buggers, with their polo mallets and their long-legged blonds, kissing in Regent's Park, my hands cupping her breasts, so nice, religious experience, actually, kind of ecstasy, puddles everywhere, and her breath on my face, the smell of her hair, her perfume, like violets.

MARCY. You're still groggy, I think.

RUFFING. I saw her on the steps. I saw her. She was so beautiful.

MARCY. (*Cradling his head in her arms.*) Easy. Just lay back and rest a minute. It's all right.

RUFFING. She looked just like you. I have your picture in my pocket watch. It's a dead woman. The loveliest creature. So gentle. When you died, I turned to stone.

MARCY. I know. I know. It's all right. (*SHE is stroking his hair*.) Dolly, bring him a small glass of wine, and don't throw it in his face.

DOLLY. I'm sorry. I'm doing the best I can. It's not my fault. I'm with child. Don't yell.

MRS. FRENCH. Nobody is yelling at you.

DOLLY. I'm very sensitive.

MRS. FRENCH. You're as dumb as a turnip.

MRS. RAVENSCROFT. Will you two stop bickering?

RUFFING. All I could think of was my daughter. I thought—I'm going to die, and she'll never know, she'll never know how desperately I love her. She'll go to her old age thinking I didn't much care one way or the other. We believe we do not investigate, you see, the truth of our own lives, we believe we investigate the truth of other lives, but not our own, never our own, and yet it always is, ultimately, you see, our own truth or lies we find, we look at the other and it's a mirror, we look in a mirror, and turn away, but it's a house of mirrors.

MRS. RAVENSCROFT. What the hell is he going on about? Is he all right? This sudden proclivity of his for philosophizing is a development I look upon with genuine alarm.

MARCY. I think he's had a mild concussion. He's not quite himself yet. That and the drinking seems to have made him slightly delusional.

MRS. RAVENSCROFT. Well, at the very least, that should improve his ability to communicate with Gillian. Probably, you know, we should take advantage of this, somehow.

MARCY. Just leave him alone.

GILLIAN. You really love your daughter, don't you, Inspector?

RUFFING. Yes. I do.

GILLIAN. My Papa loved me, too, only sometimes, sometimes he was intensely peculiar.

MRS. RAVENSCROFT. Gillian.

RUFFING. What do you mean, Gillian?

MRS. RAVENSCROFT. She doesn't mean anything.

RUFFING. Yes she does. Tell me, Gillian. What kind of peculiar?

MRS. RAVENSCROFT. My husband was not peculiar.

GILLIAN. It's just that—

MRS. RAVENSCROFT. Gillian, shut up.

MRS. FRENCH. We're going to have to tell him, you know, sooner or later.

MRS. RAVENSCROFT. Ellen—

RUFFING. Tell me what?

MRS. FRENCH. It's either that or kill him. He's not going to give up, he won't be fooled, we can't bribe him, and none of us seems quite up to killing him, so the only solution, as I see it, is just to tell him.

MRS. RAVENSCROFT. Ellen, you say one more word and you're fired.

RUFFING. Tell me what? The truth? Am I about to hear the truth? Am I at last to hear the truth?

MRS. RAVENSCROFT. Marcy, take Gillian back to her room.

RUFFING. (*Staggering to his feet.*) No. Everybody stays. Nobody moves from this room until we get to the bottom of this. Mrs. French, you were saying?

MRS. FRENCH. Mr. Ravenscroft—was a dear man, in many ways, and we all loved him, most of the time, but when he drank, he was, he was—somewhat different. He—he was fond of—he would—he liked, the truth is, he liked to—

RUFFING. To what? He liked to what?

MRS. FRENCH. To dress up.

RUFFING. Dress up? Dress up what?

MRS. FRENCH. Dress up himself.

RUFFING. Dress up himself? In what way? You mean as in military uniform?

MRS. FRENCH. Not exactly.

RUFFING. What then? Gorilla suits?

MRS. FRENCH. In dresses.

RUFFING. In dresses? Mr. Ravenscroft liked to wear dresses?

MRS. FRENCH. Well, only at night. He preferred evening wear. He used to, to walk around the house at night in them. He had a particular favorite, a white ball gown—

RUFFING. Oh, my god.

MRS. FRENCH. He particularly liked to dance about at the top of the staircase, in the middle of the night.

RUFFING. Oh, my god.

MRS. FRENCH. Yes, well, you see, he needed someone to dance with, and, um, well, that was Patrick's job.

RUFFING. This is appalling.

MRS. FRENCH. No, he was a wonderful dancer. But you see, as Mr. Ravenscroft got a bit older, he—he spread out a bit, he no longer fit properly into the ball gown, you see, and also, it had always bothered him, you know, that he wasn't the one to lead, you see. I mean, Mr. Ravenscroft was a very manly man, in every sort of way, and he preferred, on the whole, to lead, so one night, he asked Patrick if he wouldn't mind changing places with him, you know, put on the ball gown instead.

RUFFING. I find this utterly revolting.

MRS. FRENCH. Well, at first Patrick wouldn't do it. I mean, it was one thing to humor the old fool up there at night when everyone else was asleep, but it was quite another to be putting on a ball gown himself. Although I must say it did look nice on him. In any case, Patrick was a very loyal fellow, and finally he gave in. But the thing is, the thing is, it bothered him considerably, and perhaps that's what led him to be so active in the seduction department, I mean, you know, a desire to prove to himself and the rest of us that he was, you know, all right. That he didn't really like dancing with Mr. Ravenscroft in a white ball gown, but the truth is, he rather did like it. And this frightened him. So one night he refused to do it any more, and there was a great argument between the two of them at the top of the staircase, and Mr Ravenscroft got very angry and Patrick pushed him down the steps. He said it was an accident. It's true. It's bizarre, but it's true.

RUFFING. Then who killed Patrick?

MRS. FRENCH. Well, Marcy, of course.

GILLIAN. No she didn't. I did.

RUFFING. Why?

GILLIAN. Because he killed my father. He pushed him down the stairs. So I did the same to Patrick.

MRS. RAVENSCROFT. Don't listen to her, Inspector, my daughter is quite mad, she doesn't know what she's saying. It wasn't Gillian, it was Mrs. French. Can't you see she's concocted this whole ridiculous story about men dressed up in ball gowns to confuse you and lead you from the truth?

MRS. FRENCH. How dare you accuse me like that, after all I've done for you, hiding your filthy, trollopy affairs, lying for you—

RUFFING. Then you were lying.

MRS. FRENCH. I was before, but now I'm telling the truth.

RUFFING. Before when? Which time? ·

MRS. RAVENSCROFT. She is not telling the truth. My husband did not wander around the house at night wearing women's clothing.

RUFFING. Dolly, come here.

DOLLY. What?

RUFFING. Come here, I want to ask you something.

DOLLY. Don't hit me.

RUFFING. I promise not to hit you, I just want to know one thing: did Mr. Ravenscroft wander around the house at night wearing a white ball gown, or didn't he?

DOLLY. No. I don't know. Is this a trick question? Why are you asking ME?

RUFFING. Because I'm desperate for a simple answer and you are a desperately simple person. Now, did he or didn't he? Come on. Answer me.

MRS. RAVENSCROFT. Dolly—

RUFFING. Be quiet.

MRS. FRENCH. Dolly—

RUFFING. Let her alone.

DOLLY. Oh, all right, all right, I confess, I did it.

RUFFING. You did it? You did what?

DOLLY. I killed Patrick. It was all my fault.

RUFFING. How was it your fault?

DOLLY. I loved him. We were going to have a baby together. He promised he'd marry me, but then he kept putting it off. I was scared he never would. Then finally he told me he'd marry me the very next day if I'd just, if I'd just do this one thing for him.

RUFFING. Yes? What? What thing?

DOLLY. If I'd dress up in one of Mr. Ravenscroft's old suits, and dance with Patrick at the top of the staircase. Patrick had this really nice dress. It was all white, lovely, I thought it would have looked much better on me, but he made me wear the suit, and he wore the dress, and we danced. He said it was like a wedding rehearsal, but I couldn't imagine what kind of wedding it would be, with me in the suit and him in the dress, I mean, I don't think the vicar would have liked it at all. But then I don't think Patrick was really right in the head after Mr. Ravenscroft died, he was like a crazy man, humming and talking to people that wasn't there, but I was desperate, I'd have done just about anything to get him to marry me.

RUFFING. Then how did Patrick die?

DOLLY. Mr. Ravenscroft's suit was way, way too big for me, and Patrick kept dancing faster and faster, crazy, and mumbling to people that wasn't there, and whirling me around till I got very dizzy and feeling sick to my stomach with the baby and all, and I stepped on the hem of his dress and he fell down the steps and broke his neck.

MRS. FRENCH. Good Christ, girl, you mean I've been perjuring myself all this time to protect these rich people, and all this time it was just you?

DOLLY. I'm sorry, I didn't mean to, I'm a good dancer, but I never wore trousers before, and they was too big, and I'm not used to leading.

RUFFING. So when you found Patrick at the bottom of the steps, he was wearing the ball gown.

MRS. FRENCH. Yes sir.

DOLLY. I ran down the steps and saw that he was dead, and I panicked, I ran into my room and changed into my own nightclothes before anybody else came out.

GILLIAN. Does this mean I didn't kill him?

RUFFING. It would appear so. Don't you know?

GILLIAN. I don't know. I was dreaming, I was dreaming I was dancing with Patrick at the top of the stairs, and at first he was dressed in one of Papa's suits and I had on a beautiful white dress like the ghost, and then Patrick had on the dress, and then it was my papa, and then Patrick was screaming at my papa only no words came out, and then in my dream I pushed Patrick down the steps, and then I woke up, and there was a commotion on the steps, and I ran out to the top of the staircase, and there was Patrick at the bottom, and I thought I must have done it in my dream, or in my sleep, I don't know, I get these things mixed up sometimes, and then Marcy came out and saw me there and told me to go back to my room.

RUFFING. Marcy thought you'd pushed him down the stairs, didn't you, Marcy?

MARCY. It did appear that way, yes.

RUFFING. And when Mrs. Ravenscroft appeared, and found the two of you there, she thought the same thing. So after you got Gillian calmed down and Dolly had gone for the doctor, Mrs. Ravenscroft no doubt had Mrs. French change Patrick's clothing, and then took Marcy aside and arranged for her to take the blame. The hope was that it would be considered an unfortunate accident, but if it wasn't, well, Marcy was expendable, wasn't she?

MARCY. She promised to take care of my child, to bring her to England and take care of her, financially, see that she had a good home. What else could I do?

RUFFING. You could have told the bloody truth.

MARCY. And see Gillian go to prison? Or see Mrs. Ravenscroft tell everyone that I was lying, that I'd done it? Who do you think would have been believed? And what would happen to my child if I was in prison and no provision made for her future?

MRS. RAVENSCROFT. All right, Inspector, you've found your truth, such as it is, more or less, now what are you going to do with it? It doesn't really have to all come out about my husband and Patrick and the wretched ball gown and everything, does it? I don't see why. You and I can still be married. I'll be good to you. I know a few tricks, Inspector. I was brought up in India. Have you read the *Kama Sutra*?

RUFFING. I spend my entire life searching about for the truth. I give up everything for it. I earn the enduring hatred of my cretinous superiors for it. I neglect my family. I get paid less than a street sweeper. I struggle and sweat through the filth and the muck to painfully make my way to the truth. And when I get to it, it's always the same. Wretched. Pathetic. Embarrassing. Ridiculous. Appalling.

MRS. RAVENSCROFT. So stop wasting your time, Inspector. Marry a beautiful, lusty, rich young widow. Live out your days in peace and happiness here with us.

Play croquet. Play quoits. Play house. Play anything you like.

RUFFING. (*Looking at her, then at the others, a long moment. Then:*) All right. This is how it's going to be. Mrs. Ravenscroft will see to it that Dolly and her child will always have a home here, and will be provided for financially. Agreed?

MRS. RAVENSCROFT. Of course. I swear it.

RUFFING. She will also see that Marcy's child is brought here safely from the convent in Vienna, and that Marcy and her child also have a home here and financial security as long as they wish to have it. Agreed?

MRS. RAVENSCROFT. Agreed. Fine. I'll do it.

RUFFING. Fine. In that case, this is my report. Patrick Roarke had too much to drink one night and fell down the main staircase. Why he came upstairs is unknown—perhaps to try and romance the beautiful governess. But in any case, it was an accident, as of course was the earlier death of Mr. Ravenscroft. All right?

MRS. RAVENSCROFT. Thank you, Inspector.

RUFFING. Now get out of here and leave me alone. In honor of the death of my great passion for truth, I'm going to drink myself into a stupor.

MRS. RAVENSCROFT. Does this mean we're going to be married?

RUFFING. No, it most emphatically does not mean anything of the kind, and if you ever attempt to bribe me in any way again, I swear to God I'll run you in and lock you up, no matter what the consequences, is that clear?

MRS. RAVENSCROFT. Perfectly. (*Pause.*) Odd. I'm almost disappointed. Isn't that silly? Well, I'll have Mrs.

French prepare the guest room for you, Inspector. Ellen, go and do that, please, and take Dolly with you.

MRS. FRENCH. Yes mum. Come on, child.

(As MRS. FRENCH drags her into the darkness:)

DOLLY. Thank you sir. God bless you.

(Mrs. French and Dolly are gone.)

MRS. RAVENSCROFT. Come along, Gillian. It's way past your bedtime.

GILLIAN. I was right, then, wasn't I? It was the ghosts, after all. The ghosts got into Papa's head and Patrick's head and made it all happen. The ghosts haunted them to death. You're a nice man, Inspector. I'm going to have wonderful dreams about you.

(SHE comes over and kisses him on the cheek, then allows herself to be led into the shadows by MRS. RAVENSCROFT. MARCY and RUFFING are left alone.)

MARCY. That was a very kind thing you did.

RUFFING. I did myself a kindness by disposing of the entire wretched matter once and for all.

MARCY. You did your job. You found the truth.

RUFFING. Did I?

MARCY. Didn't you?

RUFFING. The investigation is one thing. What you finally settle upon is another thing. What you decide to tell others about it is yet a third thing. And what the truth really is—what the truth is—(*Pause. HE drinks.*)

MARCY. Inspector.

RUFFING. What?

MARCY. I don't think you should have any more to drink tonight.

RUFFING. Oh, you don't, do you? Why not? You think I'll get drunk and fall down the stairs? Then you can dress me up in a ball gown, that will really confuse them. Probably you people are planning on murdering me in my sleep, anyway.

MARCY. Listen, Inspector, could you possibly do me just one more kindness?

RUFFING. What's that?

MARCY. Would you—could I stay with you tonight?

RUFFING. You don't have to do that. I'll keep my word. And I'll bloody well see to it that Mrs. Ravenscroft keeps hers. We'd best get it down in writing. I have a legal friend who can work it out for you.

MARCY. I'm not talking about that.

RUFFING. Then what are you talking about?

MARCY. I'm talking about the undeniable fact of my incredible loneliness. I'm talking about the undeniable fact that I very, very much do not want to be alone tonight.

RUFFING. (*Looks at her.*) What a stupid man I am. What a monumentally stupid man I am, after all. I know nothing. I know nothing at all. (*Pause.*) I would be honored. I would consider it a great honor, to have your company tonight, or, for that matter, any other night, until judgement day. Perhaps beyond. Perhaps in fact—

MARCY. Perhaps there is even some truth in that.

(THEY look at each other. RUFFING puts his drink down. The LIGHT fades on them and goes out. Ticking CLOCKS in the DARKNESS.)

NOTES ON *RAVENSCROFT*

(1) Every play is a mystery, a riddle to be solved. Every
play is a labyrinth of motives. You begin with one
question and end perhaps with another. Or you find yourself
lost in the labyrinth of possibility. A work of art with a
simple answer is a lie. But then so must that sentence be a
lie. Inspector Ruffing believes that he is attempting to
solve one case, but in the course of his journey through the
labyrinth he discovers that every investigation is sooner or
later to become an investigation of one's own self. In the
second act, as he begins to shed his disguise as Inspector
Ruffing, he comes upon the true center of his
investigations, his own lost soul. In the center of the
labyrinth is a mirror.

(2) As a child I was fascinated by the board game called
Clue. It seemed completely self-contained, a perfect little
universe. The house felt real, the people, the murder
weapons, the atmosphere of the thing was rich, it pulled
me into a safe place, a place where danger and darkness
were under some control, there were certain rules. But
someone did kill someone, somewhere. It is a mistake to
try to parody such things—you must play them straight or
they don't work. When I was a bit older I realized that the
game was a manifestation of a sub-genre of mystery
literature, the English country house murder mystery. But
like all recurring motifs in popular literature, this one must
touch in some fundamental way some basic archetypal
pattern of needs in the human psyche. The isolation, the
fear, the mystery of death, the hidden excitement of sexual
encounters in dark rooms, the sense of danger in an old,

complex, labyrinthine haunted place. The labyrinth is the
human mind, is the old house. Again and again I find
myself writing about the insides of old houses, labyrinths
containing mysteries, places of fear that draw one. The
sense of mystery is always connected with the mystery of
woman.

(3) A Ravenscroft symbology: mystery, riddle, enigma,
conundrum, labyrinth, secret, puzzle, occult, ghost,
apparition, phantom, spirit, shade, shadow, specter. Stairs,
steps, ascent, descent, fall, exile, foreigner, banishment,
lies, deception, trick, fantasy, dream, magic, sleight of
hand, prevarication, falsehood, snow, snow white, snowy,
milky, pale, bloodless, wraith, frosty, hoarfrost,
whorefrost, darkness. Dress, clothing, boots, gown,
mackintosh, breeches, nightshirt, cowl, snood. Sex.
Breasts. Woman. Pleasure. Entrance. Tunnel. Hallway.
Cave. Trap. Climax. The raven as bird of death. Poe's bird,
Poe the father of the detective story. A croft is a small
farm, but it comes from old German words for little hill, as
in the mound of Venus, field, among dunes, that which
bends, from the Indo-European base meaning to turn, bend,
twist. The last twist of the knife.

(4) The playwright is the detective, he makes
investigations into truth. Does every mystery have a
solution? If not, must it fail as a work of art? Is an
apparent solution the only possible one? A play is a series
of questions moving towards an answer. The audience
gathers the evidence. The growing arousal must lead to a
climax, as in sex. And yet dramatic theory, like sex
manuals, pales before the mystery of the real animal. Is a

play simply a mechanism for arousing and then satisfying? To be an honest investigation into truth, must one write an unsatisfactory play, a play with no climax? But if one listens to the voices properly, not attempting to fill in the blanks mechanically, as in the playwriting manuals, but following where it leads one, no matter how strange a place that may be, then the play, if you know what you're doing and have faith, will eventually, after a journey of a few months or a few years or a couple of decades, lead you to a kind of truth. So this is the elephant's burial ground. Nothing left but bones, she said. A waste land of bones. The valley of dry bones. And yet, and yet the journey itself, being itself the destination, if pursued with courage and as much integrity as one can muster, it can defy those theories and yet in its own strange way turn out to have manifested a kernel of truth in them. A good play is an endlessly unfolding mystery. When you get to the end, you want to go back to the beginning and move once again through the labyrinth of investigation, arousal, undressing of the subject of one's desperate attention. Lady of situations, eyes of the raven. What you find is not what you expected to find. But it is what you have always known.

(5) The attempt to murder the author is an activity engaged in by cretins. In the short run, these people win. In the long run, they are the balls of dung dropped by the wild goose in the waters of Babylon.

Also by
Don Nigro...

Joan of Arc in the Autumn
The King of the Cats
Laestrygonians
The Last of the Dutch Hotel
The Lost Girl
Loves Labours Wonne
Lucia Mad
Lucy and the Mystery of the
    Vine Encrusted Mansion
Lurker
MacNaughton's Dowry
Madeline Nude in the
    Rain Perhaps
Madrigals
Major Weir
The Malefactor's
    Bloody Register
Mariner
Mink Ties
Monkey Soup
Mooncalf
Mulberry Street
My Sweetheart's The
    Man in the Moon
Narragansett
Necropolis
Netherlands
Nightmare with Clocks
November
Paganini
Palestrina
Panther
Pendragon
Pendragon Plays
Picasso
Ragnarok

Rat Wives
Ravenscroft
The Reeves Tale
Rhiannon
Ringrose the Pirate
Robin Hood
The Rooky Wood
Scarecrow
Seance
Seascape with Sharks
    and Dancer
The Sin-Eater
Something in the Basement
Sorceress
Specter
Squirrels (Nigro)
Sudden Acceleration
Sycorax
Tainted Justice
The Tale of the Johnson Boys
Tales from the Red Rose Inn
Things That Go Bump
    in the Night
The Transylvanian Clockworks
Tristan
Uncle Clete's Toad
Warburton's Cook
The Weird Sisters
Widdershins
Wild Turkeys
Winchelsea Dround
Within the Ghostly
    Mansion's Labyrinth
Wolfsbane
The Wonders of the
    Invisible World Revealed
The Woodman and the Goblins

Please visit our website **samuelfrench.com** for complete
descriptions and licensing information